A Place To Call Home

BY LACEY BLACK

*Emma ~
May all roads lead you home!
♡ Lacey Black*

Lacey Black

Copyright © 2016 Lacey Black

Cover design – Freya Barker

Editor – Kara Hildebrand

Proofreading – Joanne Thompson

Formatting – Brenda Wright, Formatting Done Wright

This book is a work of fiction. Any reference to historical events, real people, or real places are used fictitiously. Other names, characters, places and events are products of the author's imagination, and any resemblance to actual events or places or persons, living or dead, is entirely coincidental.

No part of this publication may be reproduced by any means without the prior written permission of the author.

All rights reserved.

A Place To Call Home

© Lacey Black 2016

Eight years ago, Colbi Leigh fled her safe little hometown in Kentucky and followed her dreams to New York City. She left everything behind: her parents, her brother, and the love of her life, Aiden Hughes. Now, Colbi must return home in the wake of her brother's unexpected death in Afghanistan where she's about to come face-to-face with her old demons.

Aiden has been left unsettled since his one true love left him for something else in the Big Apple eight long years ago. After the unexpected death of his oldest friend, who was serving in the Army, Aiden finally comes face-to-face with the woman who stole his heart and has haunted his dreams.

What happens when old lovers reunite in the midst of tragedy? Is it finally a happily ever after, or will their dreams tear them apart once more?

**Note to the reader: This novella is about 23,000 words and was originally published in the Honor Anthology, May 2016.

Lacey Black

Index

Chapter One 5

Chapter Two.. 15

Chapter Three.. 22

Chapter Four 35

Chapter Five.. 50

Chapter Six.. 75

Chapter Seven 85

Chapter Eight 88

Epilogue 99

Chapter One

Colbi

As the wheels of the plane finally touch down at Louisville International Airport, my heart summersaults painfully and pounds loudly in my chest. The noise is so thunderous I'm sure the pilot can hear it over the barrage of cabin noise. Under normal circumstances, flying doesn't bother me. In fact, I love flying. The ability to travel from one end of the country to the other in mere hours. The thrill-seeker in me revels being suspended thirty thousand feet above the earth, completely forfeiting control to a manmade machine and the couple of individuals operating it. And let's not forget the fact that it's a people-watcher's paradise. Establishing everyone's backstory is always one of my favorite pastimes. But not today.

Not since the phone call.

Truth be told, my heart hasn't dislodged from my throat since I received the call almost forty-eight hours ago. Nothing–and I mean *nothing*–can prepare you for that call. The one that rocks you clear down to your toes, stripping your soul of every ounce of happiness it possesses, and leaves you in a pile of despair and tears. It was that phone call that changed my life forever.

Gone.

Just like that. My brother was gone.

I quickly brush the pesky tears away, refusing to let my emotions get the best of me in the middle of a busy airport. Following along with the masses like cows being put out to pasture, I attempt once more to push all thoughts of Marcus from my mind as I make my way towards baggage claim. But those slippery little devils have stained my cheek since the moment my mom called to tell me the tragic news.

As another departure is announced for final boarding, I finally make my way to the large conveyor belt. It takes longer than normal for my beat up black suitcase to make its way towards me. In fact, I'm pretty sure my bag was the last one pulled from the belly of the jet that delivered me straight from LaGuardia to Louisville. Par for the course on this muggy, humid May afternoon.

Grabbing a hold of the bag, I fling it over the edge of the slow-moving device with enough force that I'm rewarded with a loud crack as my suitcase hits the tile floor. The bracket holding my wheel splinters into a thousand pieces, raining black plastic all over the floor in a three-foot radius. I stare down at the shattered remains of my wheel in utter disbelief. *REALLY!?*

A Place to Call Home

Why not throw in a few more rain clouds, Universe?

I oddly limp with my broken suitcase backwards until I'm against the wall, well out of the way of the other scurrying travelers. It doesn't take a brain surgeon to realize I'm totally and royally screwed. The wheel is completely gone on the left side, leaving sharp shards of black plastic sticking out at dangerous angles. There's no way I can maneuver this thing through the airport on one wheel which means I'm carrying it.

Awesome.

And to think, I almost left those last two pairs of boots at home.

Hefting the bag up with my right arm, I start to make the long trek through the masses of travelers, towards the entrance where I'm meeting my father. I'd be a liar if I said I wasn't starting to sweat. The combination of May Midwestern heat and the fifty pounds of clothes and accessories I crammed into a single suitcase are weighing on me quickly. I've barely made it twenty feet and I already have to switch arms. Of course, juggling my purse and small carry-on bag with electronics isn't an easy task when you're trying not to decapitate the person walking next to you.

Par for the course, Colbi.

Naturally, if I wasn't making the equivalent of a fast-food employee's wages, I might've been able to afford a newer suitcase that didn't look like it barely survived the seventies. My dream was simple: graduate from the Fashion Institute of Technology in New York and work my way to the top, preferably alongside a wedding gown designer in New York City. And while that dream is still very much alive and well, it has proven to be a very slow progression. Fine. I've barely climbed up from the bottom rung of the ladder.

When I graduated FIT, I was ecstatic to receive an internship with Enchanted Elegance, one of the top five wedding dress designers in the state of New York. Alana Kensington appeared to be the perfect boss: tough, yet approachable. Her custom designs were sought after by some of the most prestigious brides in the country, and I wanted just a tiny piece of that.

I knew I would start at the bottom. I knew I would have to work hard–more hours than I wanted to really acknowledge–to prove my worth. But I was dedicated. I was driven. And I was going to make it, damn it.

I just didn't realize "making it" was short for "she's got you by the balls." My internship eventually turned into full-time employment, but I was the hamster in the wheel, running as fast as I possibly could, only to not have anything to show for it at the end of the day. My title as Assistant was really code for coffee runner. Scapegoat. Receiver of daily verbal lashings. I have yet to touch a pencil in an actual Alana Kensington original, nor has Alana shown any interest in looking at the personal designs that I pour my heart and soul into. Instead, I make sure the pins are stocked, the material is flawless, the measuring tape is always within reach, and the coffee pot is full. No matter where my place is in the process, I'm still involved in helping brides with their perfect dress.

But this was my dream, right?

Stopping in the middle of the airport, I choke on the very air trying to fill my lungs. Uncontrollable tears fill my eyes, clouding my vision once more. Travelers brush past me, bumping into my arms or my broken suitcase, without even a glance back or a word of apology. I'm lost in a sea of people, drowning in despair and hurt. I choke on everything: my loss, my travel, my less-than-thrilled boss when I explained that I was rushing home to be with my family during the unexpected loss of the man just two years older than my own twenty-six years. It suddenly all becomes too much. In the middle of the crowded airport, the loss of my brother finally really hits me. And damn, does it hit me hard, like a line drive straight to the chest. I can't seem to make my legs work. Moving out of the way of the other travelers suddenly isn't even an option for me. I'm grounded, rooted right where I stand.

The bag falls to the floor, crashing in a loud heap of dead weight. Marcus. My grief overcomes me, swallowing me whole in the most excruciating pain I've ever felt. My heart shatters all over again, just like it did the moment I received that devastating phone call from my mom. But this time, the shock of that call isn't a factor. My grief grips me tightly and won't let go. The tears start to fall and won't let up. There, in the middle of the airport, I lose my grip on my carefully placed composure, and maybe a bit of reality.

Fellow travelers sidestep around me as if to get as far away as they can from the crazy girl having a meltdown in the middle of the airport. Very few glance in my direction, and the ones that do offer me a look of pity. One lady even offers me a crumpled up tissue from her pocket as she walks by. I can only give her a watery nod of appreciation as I grip the flimsy piece of tissue as if it were a lifeline before she scurries off, getting lost in the throngs of people.

My despair refuses to ease up its firm clasp, even the slightest bit. The simple task of breathing appears to be just as much of a chore as dressing was this morning. I squeeze my eyes tightly closed and count to ten in an attempt to slow my breathing. When that doesn't work, I try again. Panic starts to set in. I feel it deep in my chest as my breathing becomes more and more labored. I've never in my life had a panic attack. I gulp shallow breaths of air, but my mind is elevating quickly to panic mode. I'm going to die right here in the middle of the airport from lack of oxygen. Dear God, I'm going to die and my parents are going to bury both of their children. Together.

My eyes fly open as that image takes root in my mind. I'm surely having an out-of-body experience at this point. Maybe lack of oxygen to my brain is causing hallucinations because there before me is a vision of my past. Like the parting of the Red Sea, bodies of fellow travelers divide and reveal a tall cowboy in tight Wranglers and a worn baseball cap.

Aiden.

I choke, and he must recognize the fear and panic in my eyes. Aiden moves quickly, his legs eating up the distance between us in just a few short seconds. He looks so real–so life-like. His brown hair curls out around the edges of his baseball cap as if he has missed a recent cut. Apparently unable to squeeze in a shave this morning, his chin and strong jaw are dusted with a bit of roughness that only makes his appearance that much more handsome. Hard muscles hidden beneath a tight green t-shirt have replaced the boyish youthfulness I remember so vividly. And those eyes–damn, those hazel eyes. They're bright and shining and appear more golden than I remember. He's the best hallucination I could conjure up at this moment of weakness and pain.

But then he touches my cheek, catching the tears streaming down my face. That touch, that single graze of his rough finger against my skin, sends ripples of calmness through my body, and maybe a little ripple of something else. I gasp at the touch, refusing to take my eyes away from his. If I'm going to lose this hallucination, I want to remember the way Aiden's eyes look at this exact moment. Calm. Peaceful. Memorable.

I can't stop the loud sob that slips from my throat. It sounds foreign and hollow as it echoes off the concrete walls. It startles me to know that piercing sound came from my small body. Aiden reaches forward, gripping me tightly, and crushes my body into his. His warmth and familiarity wrap around me, soothing me instantly. The scent that I can only associate with him fills my senses, rendering me speechless and defenseless. If this is a dream, I'm pretty sure I don't ever want to wake up.

I don't know how long we stand there as travelers come and go around us. When I'm sure there aren't any more tears to possibly cry, I finally push away from Aiden's chest. His shirt is soaked through leaving very little to the imagination of what kind of man he's become. Strong. Powerful. I draw my gaze quickly up to his face. Bad idea. Those damn eyes are focused directly on me; consuming me, devouring me, eating me whole.

"Your dad was getting ready to come get you when Pastor Green showed up at the house. He didn't want to leave your mom alone to talk about the services, so he asked me to come and get ya."

I nod my acknowledgement because words seem to evade me. Wiping away the residue from my tears, I scan the crowd. Suddenly embarrassed by my emotional breakdown, I can't seem to look at him. Of course I wasn't hallucinating this whole thing and real Aiden would witness my emotional collapse in the middle of a busy international airport. Why not? The Universe hates me.

"Don't do that. Don't hide from me," Aiden says as if sensing my mortification. His eyes sparkle, even through the crappy florescent lighting of the airport. It instantly reminds me of those nights so long ago spent wrapped up in each other's arms under the glow of dashboard lights.

Aiden picks up my broken suitcase as if it didn't weigh as much as a grade schooler. "It's heavy," I tell him lamely as he reaches for my hand. The contact causes little flutters deep in the pit of my stomach. Aiden hasn't touched me in eight years. Eight very long, lonely years.

Together, we silently head towards the parking garage. Sunshine assaults my sensitive eyes as we step through the doors and into the warm day. Without another word, Aiden leads me towards a mammoth beast of a truck parked in the back row. Of course adult

Aiden would have the biggest truck imaginable. His love for big diesels was acquired early in his teen years when his dad bought their first big diesel-guzzling truck for the ranch. He drove that truck everywhere, including a few abandoned country roads where we'd park and make out like only teenagers do.

Aiden releases my hand and I feel the loss instantly. He opens up the back door and tosses my broken bag inside before opening the passenger door for me. There's a small step beneath the door, but before I can use it, Aiden wraps his warm hands around my waist and lifts, depositing me safely into the cab of his Chevy.

I look over at those familiar eyes. He appears to be assessing me. Or reading me, as if adult Aiden knows my tells as well as young Aiden did. Of course, he doesn't know me that well. Not anymore. The realization must hit him as suddenly as it hits me because he quickly drops his gaze. Aiden shuts the door and heads around to the driver's side without so much as a backwards glance.

Once inside, I still lack the ability to produce words, and apparently he's in no better condition. After a few minutes of silence, Aiden starts the truck and pulls out of the garage. The roads are familiar, even if it has been a while since I've traveled them. One thing is certain though, as I inch closer and closer to my childhood home: there's no escaping now.

Chapter Two

Aiden

The crew cab of my truck has never felt so small.

Familiarity spreads warmly through me like a shot of bourbon. Colbi is sitting in the passenger seat of my truck and the only thing I can think of is how right it feels. Her scent surrounds me, grabbing me firmly by the balls and refusing to let go. Gone is the image of her crying in my arms in the middle of the airport. Gone is the sadness of losing her brother–my best friend. Right now, the only thing I feel is contentment. Relief. Hope.

As much as I try to quash those pesky, unwelcomed feelings and brush them aside, I just can't seem to do it. This girl–now a woman–has invaded my thoughts and dreams for eight long-ass years. She will forever be the one that got away. The one I just can't seem to let go of. Maybe this is the Universe's way of helping me move on. Maybe finally coming face-to-face with Colbi Leigh will help eradicate the ghost of what-could-have-been from my life. Maybe now I can bury the past and move forward.

As unsettling as that thought is, I know it's for the best, and I grab a hold of it with everything I have. I can do this: I can move on.

Well, at least I thought I could until she speaks and those thoughts fly straight out the window along I-71. "Thank you for picking me up," she whispers. Even in the silence of my truck cab, I still strain to hear her soft words.

"No problem." It's a lame response, but I just don't know what else to say. My damn heart is pounding wildly in my chest, screaming at me to confess resurrecting feelings. *Stupid fucking organ.*

"It still seems so surreal, ya know?" I feel the heat of those mesmerizing blue eyes on me as I drive.

I try not to look her way, but eventually, the urge is too great. And *holy shit!* I feel those eyes all the way down to my toes. The sadness cuts me deep, and it takes me a few breaths to choke out my response. "I know." Again, lame.

Silence accompanies us for the remainder of the trip. As soon as we near Pleasureville, our little dinky hometown, something stirs to life in Colbi. She starts to fidget with the long, blond locks of her hair, scraping at what little nail polish remains on her nails, and continually uncrosses and re-crosses her legs. The movement draws my eyes from the roadway to the long, shapely legs that used to wrap around my waist. I'm a

A Place to Call Home

bastard for sitting in the driver's seat, lusting over my ex at a time like this. But that doesn't stop my eyes from traveling upward until they catch a peek of that smooth, creamy flesh where her thighs disappear beneath her shorts. *Damn.*

As I head down the county road that leads to the Leigh house, Colbi rolls down her window. Soft wind whips at her hair, sending it flying around the truck cab the way it used to. I hear her inhale deeply over the noise of the wind. "I forgot what fresh air smells like."

"They don't have fresh air in New York?" I ask.

"Not like this. This air is clean. New York air is…different." I nod, not trusting myself to speak, especially about such a sticky topic as New York.

"How are they?" she asks, turning and looking at me, after a brief moment of silence.

Exhaling deeply, I answer her honestly. "Not good. Your mom has done nothing but cry since she got the call, and your dad is trying to be brave and not cry in front of her. I suspect that when he goes outside to check on the dogs, he's using it to get away for a few minutes and collect his thoughts."

Colbi nods as she returns her eyes to the passing scenery. It doesn't take long before we're passing the unmistakable fields and pastures along the Leigh property. I pull into the driveway of the place that was always a second childhood home to me. Growing up with Marcus as my closest friend only ensured that I had an additional place to go for home-cooked meals and plenty of trouble. *Damn, we got into some shit together back in the day. This place won't be the same without you, buddy.*

Parking my truck at the end of the endless line of cars in the driveway, I instantly feel the change in the truck. Tension and uncertainty radiates off Colbi like a furnace. Turning off the ignition, I wait to take a cue from her as she stares at the home she was born in; the home she ran away from and rarely returns to.

"Why don't you go on in and I'll grab your bag," I say, breaking the silence.

"I don't know if I can go in there." My heart practically rips in two all over again. Her words are like a knife thrust deep into my gut. Of all the things I wanted for Colbi, *this* was never one of them. Happiness. Laughter. Maybe even love someday, even if it wasn't with me. Not this fear and sadness that seems to pour from her like a faucet in the wake of her brother's death. I'd give anything just to see that beautiful smile on her face one more time.

"Sure you can; when you're ready. You were always one of the toughest, bravest, and most fearless girls I knew, Rainbow." The old nickname spills from my lips so easily that my breath hitches in my tight chest. Colbi's wide eyes slam into mine as realization grabs hold. Her lips look soft and oh-so-fucking inviting as she gapes at me from across the cab. I'm a complete bastard, I know, but the only thing I can think about is kissing her; devouring those perfect lips the way I used to all those years ago.

Bright blue eyes smile back at me, even though her mouth doesn't. "Thank you." The words are meaningful and firm. Colbi exhales slowly before turning back to the house. "I guess we better get inside, huh?"

"Whenever you're ready," I reply.

Colbi has the passenger door open before I can get around to the other side. I help her climb down from my truck, careful not to let her body slide along mine, even though I crave it more than anything. When I purchased this truck, I knew it would be difficult for women to get up in it, but that didn't bother me one bit. I saw that as an excuse to put my hands on them while I was gentlemanly enough to help them climb inside the cab. Little did I know that I really wouldn't be helping too many women climb up in the truck. Not that there hasn't been anyone interested in a ride, I guess I've just been too busy to give it my full attention. A couple of girls here and there, but none that stuck.

None like Colbi.

The slamming of a screen door draws our attention to the house. Mr. Leigh looks as if he's aged another ten years in the few hours I've been gone to pick up Colbi.

The lines around his eyes are more pronounced, his hair looks a bit grayer, and he appears as if he hasn't slept in days. But it's the smile that crosses his lips that has my attention now. It's the first glimpse of happiness that I've seen in days, and it's all directed straight at his daughter.

Without so much as a glance back, Colbi starts to walk. Her steps quickly turn into a run as she nears the front porch, flies up the steps, and launches herself into her dad's awaiting arms. The tears I've witnessed Scott Leigh fight for the last few days finally pour, unchecked, down his cheeks. Their joint sobs echo off the worn floorboards and tired shutters. It's agonizingly hard to witness, but I know that they both need this moment. They both need to find comfort in each other's arms as father and daughter. It's a harsh gut-check of a reminder knowing that I'm no longer a part of this picture. And I haven't been for quite some time.

"Come on, baby girl. Let's get you inside where it's cool. Your mom really needs you right now," Scott says hoarsely. Colbi only nods her acknowledgement as she wipes tears from her eyes. With a quick look back in my direction, Colbi turns and heads into the house.

When the screen door slams behind her, I turn my attention back to Scott. "Thank you for grabbing her," he says, oblivious to my inner turmoil.

"No problem," I reply casually.

Scott looks at me long and hard before offering me a knowing smile. Okay, so maybe he's not so oblivious. "You coming inside?" he asks as I carry Colbi's broken suitcase towards the porch.

"Naw, I think I'll head home and check on the horses. You guys need some time to yourselves."

Scott nods once more. "You know you're always welcome here, Aiden. You're a part of this family, too."

Emotions lodge in my throat and tears burn my eyes. Scott Leigh is a good man. He has always been a solid figure in my life, but never more so than these past five years since my own father's unexpected death. "I'll see ya soon. Call if you need me," I state as I deposit the bag on the porch next to him.

"Thank you." Those two words mean more than just a general statement of appreciation. Thank you for my help, sure, but thank you for caring for and looking after his family as my own. Thank you for loving his son *and* daughter. And fuck if I don't realize as I stare back up at his light blue eyes that are the spitting image of both of his children's, that I'm still gone. Eight years hasn't changed a damn thing. Her smile, her laughter, her touch. It still consumes me. I'm still completely enamored with Colbi Leigh.

Damn it all to Hell.

Chapter Three

Colbi

Walking up the stairs of the small home I grew up in is a bit surreal. After a heart wrenching, and extremely tearful reunion with my mom, I find myself completely exhausted. Falling onto my bed and sleeping for the next two days is looking better and better with each step I take.

I'm sure the extra weight on my chest has nothing to do with one Aiden Hughes. Seeing him standing in the middle of the busy airport was both shocking and comforting. His strong jaw was more pronounced and dusted with dark stubble. His eyes were the same, though, and every bit as intoxicating as they were way back when. But it was his build that surprised me the most. Aiden was always a strong kid, working hard on his parents' horse ranch, but he always had a lean build from years of playing high school baseball. Aiden today is thick and hard with bulging muscles that flex naturally beneath his tight t-shirt. He's no longer the boy I remember. He is one hundred percent all man. Oh, the years have definitely been good to Aiden Hughes.

When I turn at the top of the stairs, I stare ahead at four doors. On the right, doors that lead to my parents' bedroom and the bathroom. On the left, two identical doors: one for me and the other for Marcus. I bypass the first door, glancing in and noticing my beat up suitcase sitting on the bed, and head straight for the open door at the end of the hallway.

Time stands still as I enter my brother's bedroom. The old Faith Hill poster still adorns the wall next to one of a scantily clad swimsuit model. A mess of CDs litter the desktop, and a pair of well-worn running shoes sits on the floor in front of the closet. But it's the GO ARMY t-shirt that draws my attention. Thrown over the desk chair, it's positioned perfectly as if just waiting for the owner to come home and toss it on.

But its owner isn't coming home.

Taking a few tentative steps into the room, I grab that worn, green t-shirt. Gripping it tightly in my hands, I bring the soft material up to my face, inhaling the fresh scent of fabric softener. Wet spots litter the material of the shirt my brother used to wear. I can't stop the sob that erupts from my chest, the shirt firmly locked in my clutches, as I take a single step towards the bed my brother used to sleep in.

I climb on the bed without even removing my shoes. Tucking myself into a tight ball, I cradle the shirt against my face and breathe in the sweet smell of

Marcus. The material holds only the faintest scent of his cologne. Still, after many months of his absence, I can feel him, smell his presence in this room.

He can't be gone.

I snuggle against the shirt as exhaustion finally starts to pull me under. Even though I'm in desperate need of a shower, I close my eyes and let the sweet memories of my brother lull me to sleep.

* * *

The sound of distant voices wakes me from a fitful sleep. My head feels heavy and my body lethargic as I try to get my bearings. It only takes me a moment to remember falling into a crying heap atop Marcus' bed. As the start of a headache sets in, I can instantly tell this nap did me not one ounce of good. If anything, I feel worse. Still clutching Marcus' t-shirt, I slip into the bathroom for something for the pounding in my head before going downstairs to face whatever lies ahead.

After two hours of chatting with visitors in my parents' living room, it was time to get away. Everyone has been very cordial–almost too much so–with their twenty questions about New York and my life outside of Pleasureville, but if I have to look at another pair of eyes filled with pity, over a homemade cheesecake, I was gonna snap.

A Place to Call Home

I find my mom staring off into space in the kitchen, the water from the tap running over the glass she's filling. "Mom?" I ask, startling her out of whatever memory she is lost in.

"Oh," she says, pulling the glass out from under the running water and turning off the faucet. She pours a bit from the glass and greedily drinks the water. My mom has always preferred tap water over the cold bottled water you'll find in the fridge right now. "Sorry, I was lost in thought." Her smile is small, but warm.

"I'm going to head out back for a while. I need to get out of here," I tell her honestly.

Mom's eyes crinkle a bit with laughter. "I wish I could go with you," she whispers with a wink. "If I have to eat another cinnamon roll, I might slip into a sugar coma." We've had an endless stream of friends stop by, delivering casseroles and desserts along with their condolences.

As I head towards the back door, Mom adds, "Take the flashlight by the door. It's getting late." I grab the well-used flashlight and head out into the night.

Even with the mid-May humidity, the evening air is still cool and goose bumps pepper my exposed limbs. A sweatshirt probably would have been the wiser choice, considering I'm still wearing the jean shorts and wrinkled blue tank top I arrived to town in. However, I'm not risking getting sucked back into the vortex of drugstore perfume and mothballs from the gaggle of Thursday night church group ladies inside the living room just to grab a hoodie. I will power through.

I refrain from turning on the light, opting to find my way along the familiar path, guided only by the moon. What was once a worn trail leading to the small pond behind our property is now overgrown with tall grass and weeds. My legs itch instantly from the contact, but I keep going through the foliage until I see the reflection of the moon off the small pond.

Dropping like a brick, I sit on the soft grass along the water's edge. This spot was always my favorite place in the whole world. Here, along this very pond, wrapped in someone's warm embrace, I discovered plenty in my youth. I found an escape from my parents and the stresses of life as a teenager. I found my first love. I even made it for the first time right here. Of course, there were dozens of times that followed that first time, in this very spot, wrapped in a soft fleece blanket and showered by starlight.

I sigh deeply, losing myself in the solitude of the night. Crickets chirp and frogs croak in the stillness. No car horns. No traffic zipping by. No busy sidewalks with shoulder-to-shoulder people. And certainly not a skyscraper as far as the eye can see–and then some. Just peace and quiet and an opportunity to get lost in your thoughts.

A Place to Call Home

A twig snaps off to my left and startles me. If this were New York, I would have had my pepper spray out and on the cusp of a scream at the first sign of danger, but here in the boonies, I know I don't have to react with the same level of alarm.

"Sorry, I didn't mean to scare you." The voice is gravelly and low, yet so soothing at the same time. In fact, if I were being honest here, that damn voice stirs something to life deep down inside me that I haven't felt in a long time.

"It's okay. I just thought I was alone." My heart rate kicks up a few hundred beats per minute. I'm sure Aiden can hear it from several feet away.

"What are you doing out here?" In the moonlight, I see him walk through the tall grass about ten feet away and make his way over to me.

"I just needed to get away for a bit, and this was always one of my favorite places." This pond technically belongs to Aiden's family. It's positioned about two hundred yards back where his family property meets ours. "You?" I ask as he drops down to the ground next to me.

Even in the darkness, I can see him shrug his shoulders. "I like to come here. That's all." His eyes evade mine as he gazes out at the still water.

We're both quiet for several minutes. A shiver rakes over my body as the cool air kisses my skin. "You should have a jacket," he says.

Before I can say anything, Aiden is removing his red flannel shirt and drapes it across my shoulders. The soft material warms me, enveloping me in his scent. It's potent and intoxicating. It's heaven.

"Thank you." The words are quiet and come out choked, and I'm rewarded with a nod.

Having Aiden this close to me again after all these years is messing with my head. The first thing I want to do is lean over and rest my head against his shoulder, just like I used to do when we'd sit along the water's edge. I long to feel his arm wrap around me, pulling me closer, moments before he'd tilt my chin upward and devour my lips with his. He stole my breath every time, and so much more, in the quiet of night beside the pond.

As a teenager, late at night, after my parents were off to bed and the house was still, I used to slip quietly down the stairs and out the back door. Aiden was always waiting when I made my escape to the pond out back, often with a worn red flannel blanket. The two-year age difference never mattered. It was always Aiden. He was the only thing that mattered. Together, under the moonlight, we would lie entwined and share everything from our dreams to our bodies. I don't know if my parents–or Aiden's–knew about our trysts, but no one ever said anything. In fact, Aiden was as much a part of my family as my brother Marcus, and I was a part of his as well.

"I know this is long overdue, but I'm sorry about your dad." I let the sadness of Jack's passing consume me once more. Staying away from Pleasureville, not running straight home to be with Aiden, had been the hardest thing. I longed to be with him, absorb his pain as if it were my own. And it was my own. I mourned him from afar that fall five years ago. Even though we hadn't been together for three years at that time, I ached for Aiden and wanted nothing more than to help him cope with his father's death.

"Thank you," he says. "It was a hard time for my mom."

"Marcus had told me that she found him?"

"Yeah, he went out to the north track to work with one of the new fillies they had just purchased. When he didn't come back inside for dinner, Mom went out to check on him and found him. The doc thinks the massive heart attack killed him before he hit the ground."

Without giving it a single thought, I reach over and grab Aiden's hand. His skin is warm and calloused as I link my fingers within his, offering as much comfort as I can, letting them rest on the grass between us. "I'm sure it was hard on you, too."

"Yeah," he says, clearing his throat. "I wasn't home when it happened. I should have been, but I wasn't."

"Aiden, you couldn't have done anything even if you were home."

"I know that now. I blamed myself for a long time, though." His golden eyes focus on something off in the distance.

"He was a great man. I really loved him," I tell him honestly, swallowing over the painfully large lump stuck in my throat. I fight the tears that burn my eyes, concentrating hard on a large rock not too far off in the distance. The emotions of sadness and grief aren't foreign to me. I've been consumed by them for the last two days.

"He really loved you, too. We all did," Aiden says. *Did*. That one word strikes me so deeply that I know I'll feel it forever. So final.

I feel that intense gaze lock on my face. Turning my head, I'm suddenly breathless, caused by the look of longing in his eyes. He looks as if he wants to devour me with his lips and remind me of how talented he was with those strong hands. And I'm suddenly completely on board with that entire concept.

No. You. Aren't!

Clearing my throat and desperately grasping for a redirect, I ask, "So, is there someone special waiting at home for you?"

Wait, what?

What in the hell would possess me to ask such as loaded question? Deep down I want to know, yet I'm terrified at the same time to hear the truth. Terrified that he has finally moved on. Terrified that it'll be over once and for all. And that just makes me a selfish witch because it has been eight years since I left. Since *I left him!*

Maybe this is what I need. Confirmation that Aiden has finally moved on with his life. Maybe that'll help me to finally close this epically long chapter in my life and start something new. Sure, I've tried dating over the years, but no one stuck. No one made my heart skip a beat or my toes curl from a delicious kiss the way Aiden always did.

"Naw, no one special," Aiden says with a chuckle.

"Marcus said you were seeing Mary Ellen not that long ago," I say, confessing that I had asked my brother about his best friend. On more than one occasion.

"Yeah, well, she's a nice girl and all, but there just isn't that spark. No heat." His words are punctuated with desire, heat flaring to life deep in those golden hazel eyes. I suddenly become very aware of how near Aiden is. The air is sticky in my throat and my blood starts to pump recklessly through my body. I'm caught between reality and a memory as longing starts to take over. I look down at our linked hands, watching as he tenderly strokes his thumb over my flushed skin, completely enamored with his gentle touch.

"I remember her. She was a year older than me in school, and always seemed like a sweet girl. Class president, worked with rescued animals, volunteered for everything. Nice," I whisper hoarsely.

"Yeah, well maybe I desire someone with a bit more of an edge. Someone who challenges me and likes to fly by the seat of her pants. Someone who is fearless and a bit wild. Someone who will jump naked into the pond in December after losing a bet or who talks smack for days because she is sure she can learn to drive a stick using my old man's '77 Chevy."

My eyes cloud with unshed tears. I know exactly who he's talking about. He's describing me. He has always described me with the same adjectives. Fiery. Passionate. Reckless. Ten years ago, it was those traits that caused us to crash into each other's arms. It was also the thing that drove us apart two years later.

Memory lane is a bitch sometimes, and right now is no exception. Being here–in Pleasureville–and damn near wrapped in Aiden's arms makes me want and question everything. Every damn decision I've made over the past eight years. And right now, it's just too much.

Wiping a stray tear that leaks from the corner of my eye, I turn to Aiden. "I should get back up there."

A Place to Call Home

Standing, I look down at the boy I used to love. "Thank you for keeping me company."

Aiden doesn't say anything, just gives me a nod.

Turning and heading up the path, I only make it about ten feet before I look back. His head is down, his shoulders sagging. It's as if the weight of losing his best friend is catching up with him. Hell, I'm sure having me back for the first time in nearly a decade isn't helping either. Before I can chicken out, I ask, "Are you going to be here tomorrow night?"

Aiden turns and looks over his shoulder. Moonlight reflects off those beautiful eyes. "Do you want me to be here tomorrow night?"

"Yes," I whisper honestly.

"Then I wouldn't miss it for the world."

And with that, I turn and head up the path, back towards my house. I don't look back, but I don't have to. I can feel his eyes on me the entire way.

When I reach the back door, I realize Aiden's flannel is still draped over my shoulders. It's funny that I didn't notice the extra accessory before now, but wearing something of Aiden's, after returning from the pond, is like second nature. I frequently came home in his sweatshirt or flannel. Usually, I stole it. No, it wasn't anything too devious. Aiden was well aware that he went home with less clothes than he arrived in. I used to sleep in his shirts. They always carried the scent of his deodorant and fresh air, and it was the only way to sleep with him through the night without physically having him beside me.

Oh well. All the more reason to make sure I revisit the pond tomorrow night to return the shirt and to express my gratitude.

But tonight?

Tonight I'll wrap myself in comfort. Tonight I might actually get real sleep. The first real sleep I've had since Marcus died.

Tonight I sleep with the scent of Aiden wrapped around me.

Chapter Four

Aiden

Fours days. Colbi has been home for four days, and I'm just not sure I will survive the remaining eight.

Yesterday was Marcus's funeral. It fucking sucked. The possibility of someday burying my oldest friend wasn't even a blip on my radar throughout his military career. Sure, deep down, way in the back of my mind, I knew it was possible. Hell, even he knew it was possible. One doesn't enlist in the Army without having it cross your mind a time or two, but ten years in and with an end date on the horizon from his third deployment overseas, neither of us really thought it would happen.

But it did.

I stood up with his parents, his sister's hand firmly latched onto mine as if it were the very air she needed to breathe, while the entire town paid their respects. It was all a blur; three hours of condolences and shared stories. Everyone knew him and everyone loved him. A local hero taken way too soon by a roadside bomb.

During the eulogy that I was asked to give, I fought to keep from completely losing my shit. It was the most difficult thing I've ever done; far more difficult than enduring my own father's funeral five years ago. I recounted a few stories from our wilder teen years and even finally shared the details on what happened the night the tractor ended up in the pond. Karen grinned and Scott's eyes crinkled with laughter as I finally confirmed what they'd already known: two crazy teenagers took the ol' tractor for a spin and drove it straight into the pond.

A Twenty-One Gun Salute rang through the sky, followed by the playing of Taps. The symbol of our freedom–the very thing my best friend died protecting– was folded and presented to Karen and Scott. It was my first taste of a military funeral and there was nothing like it. Somber and respectful, tearful yet a celebration of a wonderful man, it was just the way it should be. Standing alongside my best friend's final resting place, with my arms wrapped firmly around his little sister, I silently repeated the vow I made to him almost a decade ago: to always love and protect Colbi. I was finally able to let go of the tears I had been holding back since I got the call. I finally allowed myself to grieve his loss, and damn, will I feel this one deep in my gut–in my heart– for a long time. There will never be another Marcus Leigh. Not even close. Not by a long shot.

Colbi and I have met up at the pond every night. We share stories of Marcus, of her life in New York, and of mine here at home. I've been able to catch glimpses of what her life is like without me in it. Yet, we've been tiptoeing around the hard details. I don't know if she has a boyfriend. I don't know if she's as happy there as I've always wanted her to be. I don't know if she's ever regretted her decision or wondered what could have been. I stay as far away from those topics as humanly possible as if they were live grenades with the pins pulled.

I can feel her presence before I hear her. It's a calm Saturday night, with stars shining brightly as far as the eye can see, when Colbi makes her way down the worn path. I'm sitting on an old flannel blanket that I borrowed from my mom. The same one I used to carry with me back in school when I would sneak down here to steal a few kisses from her lush lips; and when I was extra good, I was rewarded with a bit more.

She drops down on the blanket. Without even thinking, I remove my zip-up jacket and drape it over her slender shoulders. Colbi slips her arms through the sleeves, covering her fitted blue t-shirt with my clothes. Tonight she has paired it with barely-there cut-off shorts that do amazing things for her mile-long legs. Those shorts also do wonders for the tightness in my own pants, which are suddenly three fuckin' sizes too small.

"Better day?" The question is as natural as breathing.

"Better day," she confirms. "It seems like the first day leading towards a new norm for Mom and Dad, you know?"

"Yeah, I know. Oh, speaking of parents, my mom wants to know if you'd come over for dinner tomorrow night. She wanted to talk to you more yesterday, but it wasn't the right time or place," I say, referring to my mom's maternal hovering over Colbi during the visitation.

"That sounds nice," she says softly. After a few pregnant pauses, she asks, "Will you be there?"

"She's making manicotti. Of course I'll be there."

"Manicotti? That's my favorite!" she exclaims. "I haven't had it since I left," she says with that bright smile and warm blue eyes that make my dick twitch. Then, as suddenly as the smile appeared, it's washed away and replaced with a look of uneasiness.

It's not a topic we've talked about yet, but it's one that needs broaching. There's so much that has been left unsaid, but maybe actually voicing some of those thoughts might aid in the moving on process. Fuck knows nothing else has helped at this point. No amount of alcohol, women warming my bed, or time has done the job.

But tonight isn't going to be that night.

"So, um, when we're done with dinner, do you think you can show me around the farm? Your mom mentioned yesterday that you've made a lot of positive improvements in the last few years. She's so proud of you for picking up where your father left off and continuing the horse farm."

"It's the only place I have ever pictured myself," I tell her without giving it any thought. Then my words seem to permeate the lust-filled fog that only Colbi seems to induce. That picture for my life was the main cause for worry where our relationship was concerned. She saw herself somewhere else and I saw myself here.

"You fit here."

Awkward silence ensues once again before I take pity on her. "Anyway, yes, you can have a tour of the farm. I'll even show you my favorite part."

"What's that?" she asks, those crystal blue eyes gleaming with anticipation.

"A little place I built out behind the pasture over there. Those trees?" I ask, pointing to the timber behind our furthermost pasture and smaller horse barn. Her head nod encourages me to continue. "It's back in there about a hundred yards. You can't see it from the barns. The timber is thick and shaded until you get to the clearing I made."

"You built a house? That's amazing." Her sweet, honey-dripped voice holds so much wonder and awe that it practically stops my heart from beating. Longing races through my body, and is quickly followed by a hot case of desire.

And just like that, I want Colbi in my house. I want her in my bed. I want her embedded into every ounce of my life so fucking fiercely that it practically steals my breath along with my sanity.

"It took me a long time since I did most of it myself, but I'm happy with it. If you want to see it, we can go after dinner." I give her a casual shrug, but my insides are anything but. I'm coiled and wound tight with anxiety and nerves at the prospect of having her in my space. The one person I thought would *never* set foot within my domain is asking for a tour. I shouldn't care what she thinks, but suddenly her opinion matters more than anything.

Ain't that the kicker? The one thing I did for myself after she left and I suddenly crave her approval.

"Thank you. I can't wait to see it." Her eyes reflect something I'm not prepared to dissect yet.

"Lie back," I tell her, stretching the blanket out behind her.

Colbi looks over at me with hesitation and a bit of curiosity in her eyes. It's as if she suddenly isn't sure she can trust herself in my presence. Well, welcome to the fucking club, sweetheart. I'm not sure if I trust myself right now, either. "Trust me," I find myself saying, despite the lack of it I feel.

A Place to Call Home

When she lies back completely, I do the same. "Let's see if you remember how to do this, Rainbow. What's that?" I ask, point up to a cluster of stars in the sky.

"Easy. That's a bowl of mac and cheese."

"Mac and cheese, huh? I think it's clearly a dog chasing a squirrel."

"A squirrel? That's not a squirrel, Aiden. Clearly, you need more practice at this. That is a chocolate chip cookie."

"Mac and cheese and a chocolate chip cookie, you say? Well, I guess we'll just have to agree to disagree on that one. What about that?" I ask, pointing to a small cluster directly overhead.

"That's a vanilla milkshake with caramel on the top."

"You might be right, but I'm sensing a pattern here. Are you hungry?"

"Apparently, I could go for something sweet," she says with a chuckle.

"One more," I state, looking up at the night Kentucky sky. "There." I point to a large group with the subtle blinking light of a jet flying high in the middle.

"A rainbow."

That one word brings back every memory I've ever had in bright Technicolor. Her nickname. The one I gave her after our first round of stargazing when she insisted that the first cluster of stars resembled a rainbow. As a young man–shit, I was a horny teenager–she was my happiness, even through the darkness or the rain. She was there, beckoning me like a dazzling rainbow. *My* rainbow.

"A rainbow," I confirm, though I'm not sure how I get the words out through my parched throat.

Turning, I find her eyes on me. I don't know who moves first–her or me–but the next thing I know, my lips taste hers. Eight years evaporate into thin air. Time stands still. My heart lurches wildly in my chest.

We're both timid at first, both fearful to move, but lust takes over automatically as I slide my rough lips over her much softer ones. Colbi turns and my arms wrap around her, pulling her closer. My tongue slips out, running along the seam of her mouth. She opens for me instantly. Colbi tastes like honey and temptation. She tastes like fucking heaven, and it takes every ounce of control I can muster to not grind my rigid dick against her stomach.

When my tongue slips inside the warmth of her mouth, my entire body flares to life with something I haven't felt in a long time. It's so much more than sexual. It's familiarity. It's as if my body is recognizing its equal. Its partner.

My hands seem to have a mind of their own when they spear roughly into those long blond locks I used to love so damn much. Hell, who am I kidding? I still love her hair. The silky softness. The smell. It's my favorite damn smell in the entire world.

Gently anchoring her to me by gripping her head, I move her slightly to give me better access, and then I go in for the kill. My tongue plunders, my lips devour, my body craves. Her. Only her. I'm alive and hungry, consumed for the first time in so long.

Colbi's hands wrap around me, clawing and gripping at my shirt. When her fingers come in contact with hot skin, I all but come in my pants like a teenager. The deep moan I swallow with my mouth does nothing to ebb my desire for her as she strokes my heated flesh with those long fingers.

Trailing open-mouthed kisses down the column of her neck, I inhale her scent. Fresh cotton and jasmine. My dick is so damn hard in my pants that I could hammer nails. Throwing her leg over my hip, Colbi grinds her core against my hardness, emancipating a deep groan of pure torture from my throat.

"You're killing me, Rainbow," I tell her as I lick and suck the wildly beating pulse point on her neck.

"Aiden." That single word a tortured groan–a plea.

"Stay still," I say, removing my lips from her neck only long enough to find the button and zipper on her shorts.

As I open the denim, I'm greeted by the smallest pair of blue cotton panties. If I wasn't already on the ground, the sight would have brought me to my knees. The material is wet and so damn arousing. Cotton has never looked so fucking good.

Sliding my hand into the open V of her shorts, I risk a glance back up at her beautiful face. Her breathing is erratic and her eyes cloudy with desire. Her blond hair is splayed out across my arm and the blanket, and I'm sure I'll never forget the way she looks right now.

With my eyes glued to hers, I slip my hand into her shorts. Gently stroking the wet material, Colbi practically jackknifes off the blanket. No one has ever responded to my touch the way she does. Within seconds, she's throwing restraint out the window and grinds against my fingers, seeking out any ounce of relief she can find.

It's a tight fit with her shorts still around her hips, but I'm able to slide my hurried fingers underneath the front panel of her panties. When I'm met with smooth, slick skin, I have to fight against the release my own body is craving. Colbi purrs as my fingers slip between the hot folds of her pussy. The look in her eyes is one of pure abandon.

I return my lips to her neck, sucking and kissing her skin, while my pointer finger slips inside her wetness. Heaven. Fucking heaven on earth right here. Her breath catches loudly in the night as I slide a second finger inside.

Years ago, I was Colbi's first everything. First kiss. First love. First lover. She was always so ungodly tight I almost blew my load the moment I was seated deep inside her. And right now, I'm transported right back to those first few times. Her tightness surrounds me, gripping me and refusing to let go.

Colbi rides my hand as I move my fingers steadily in and out of her body. I know she's close without looking at her because her body is latching onto mine with everything it has.

"Let go," I whisper against the softness of her neck. The scruff of my chin scours her skin as she lets go, coming fiercely on my fingers.

As she rides the waves of euphoria, I pepper her neck with soft, sensual kisses. The kind of kisses reserved for your love. The kind I always bestowed upon her.

Colbi shivers against me as I remove my fingers from her shorts. Her body is placid in my arms, just the way I always liked her. Spent. Exhausted in the best sort of way. Of course, the throbbing in my pants is a painful reminder that I have yet to join her in the sexual haze of pure orgasmic bliss.

But I won't be joining her. Not tonight.

"What did we just do?" she whispers. Looking up, I see her eyes closed tightly, fighting the tears that are no doubt bubbling at the surface.

"Nothing either one of us didn't want to do," I remind her.

Tear-filled blue eyes slam into mine with the force of a punch. She looks completely torn between heaven and hell. Torn between a post-orgasm stupor and worry about what happens next. What this means for either of us. Both of us.

"Don't worry about anything right now, Rainbow. Just enjoy this moment."

I pull her against me, her back to my front. My dick is still rigid in my pants and probably will be for some time. There aren't enough cold showers in Kentucky to offer the relief I need for this hard-on. No doubt, I'll be spending a fair amount of alone time in the shower this evening.

Tucking her against my body, I position her so that her ass isn't rubbing against my pants, and I hold her. It takes a few minutes before I hear the telltale sign of crying. The Colbi I knew wasn't a crier. The Colbi I remember was fierce and determined. But this Colbi has been rocked to the core. First with the loss of her brother, and now with the dozens of unanswered questions at the hands of me–no pun intended. Questions that I don't have answers to.

"I'm sorry I upset you," I whisper into her hair.

"It's not you, Aiden. It's me," she replies through her tears. *Huh, where have I heard that line before?*

"Let's not let anything that happened tonight get to us. We're friends, Colbi. Always have been and always will be. What happened tonight isn't something for you to worry about. I care about you. Let's just look at it as a friend helping a friend," I say with a smile.

Her soft chuckle is music to my ears. "A friend helping a friend, huh? Well shouldn't a friend return the favor for her friend?" she asks, scooting back until her sweet ass is pressed tightly against my throbbing erection.

"No, the friend doesn't need to return the favor," I tell her as I kiss the side of her head and scoot back. Fuck, I'm still just a man. A very horny man. "Your friend just needs to go take a cold shower. A lot of cold showers," I add, laughing.

Colbi flips over quickly so that she's facing me. Her ocean blue eyes are filled with contentment and wonder. "Thank you," she says moments before her lips gently graze mine. It's a soft kiss, a friendly kiss.

"It was my pleasure," I tell her with another quick peck.

"No, I'm pretty sure it was mine," she says, her eyes sparkling with mischief.

My laughter comes from deep in my gut, and I realize I haven't laughed like this in a while. A long while.

I decide right then and there to hold Colbi for as long as she'll let me. She fits perfectly against me, her head resting just beneath my chin. I've forgotten how much I like her hair tickling my nose as I inhale her fragrance.

"I should go," she whispers without moving. I grunt in response.

She pulls away slowly and sits up, still facing me. "Can…can I still come over to dinner tomorrow night and get that tour and stuff?" she asks hesitantly, as if the things we've shared in the last hour have somehow changed the course of our weekend.

"Mom would be disappointed if you didn't," I say. "And I would be too."

Her smile is small but still lights up the night. "Then I'll see you tomorrow?"

"Tomorrow," I confirm.

Colbi leans forward and places a tentative kiss on my lips. While I'd give anything to deepen the kiss, pull her back down to the blanket, and do all the dirty things flashing through my sex-deprived mind, I remain perfectly still.

The chaste kiss ends way too soon, but the look in her eyes tells me all I need to know about what is going

A Place to Call Home

through her mind. I see it all: her confliction, her desire, and even her love. She still feels everything I'm feeling. And I'm no longer in any position to deny or fight it.

As she walks back up the path, still wearing my shirt, I know without a doubt that I love her. I've always loved her and I always will.

But the question remains: what will I do about it?

Chapter Five

Colbi

"I'm so full, you might have to wheelbarrow me out of this room," I groan, looking down at what's left of my second helping of manicotti.

"Girl, I think you can afford a few more meals like that. Do they not feed you in New York City?" Aiden's Mom, Becky, says with a cheeky grin.

Becky looks exactly the same as she did eight years ago. Her brown hair is cut in a short bob and doesn't show any signs of gray. Her short frame is nothing like her son's, proving that Aiden got his size from his father. And as always, her smile is warm and motherly. Yearning takes root deep in my chest as the realization of what I've missed these past several years sets in.

"I eat plenty," I tell her. "In fact, when I got to New York, I think I gained fifteen pounds the first month. It didn't take me long at all to realize that my suddenly too-small pants were a result of eating takeout from every corner café or bistro in the neighborhood. Clearly my newly acquired eating habits weren't being kind to my hips."

A Place to Call Home

"Well, I'm just teasing you, sweet girl. You look amazing. Doesn't she look amazing, Aiden?" Becky asks, her face anything but innocent.

Aiden clears his throat, clearly not amused with his mother for putting him on the spot. "She looks breathtaking. Like always." The look he gives me sends heat flooding to my core and my breath stalling in my throat.

"I suppose you're both too full for dessert?" Becky smirks as she gets up to start clearing the table.

"I couldn't even eat another bite," I mumble as I throw my napkin on my plate.

"Well, how about you go take that tour and when you come back, you can have some warm apple dumplings over ice cream."

My mouth instantly starts to water as I picture the warm, gooey dessert that I used to love so much. In fact, it was Jack's favorite dessert too. It was one of the things that bonded me so quickly to Aiden's father. We were both huge fans of her homemade apple dumplings served over freshly churned ice cream.

I glance over at the empty chair at the head of the table and my gut clenches. It still doesn't seem possible that Aiden's father isn't going to be joining us for dessert. It's as if I still expect the robust man to burst through the door any minute, offering a kiss to his wife

51

as he explains that a colt was misbehaving and that's why he was late.

Slow movements draw my attention away from the empty chair. Aiden's warm hand wraps around mine, offering a gentle squeeze of comfort. The look in his eyes lets me know he feels the exact same way. Even though he's had years to deal with his father's sudden death, it still doesn't get any easier. And I know that we'll both feel the same way in regards to Marcus. I'll feel his unexpected loss for the rest of my life.

Blinking back tears, I stand up and grab the remaining plates. "Let me help with the dishes," I offer as I follow her into the kitchen.

"Absolutely not. You are my guest," she says while taking the plates from my hands and setting them down on the countertop. "Besides, Aiden mentioned that he was going to give you a tour of the farm. So, go. Enjoy."

Her eyes smile at me as she clasps my hands. Aiden comes in a few moments later and sets the rest of the dishes in the sink. "I'll just run and use the restroom, and then we can go," he says.

"It's so good to have you back here," she says, pulling me tightly into a hug after her son leaves the room. I don't have the heart to tell her that I'm only around for another week. And then I'm off again. Back to New York City. Back to my lonely little apartment

A Place to Call Home

where no one knows me. Back to the life I've found myself questioning more and more just recently.

"It's good to see you again," I tell her honestly as I choke on an unexpected onslaught of raw emotions.

"Sweet girl, sometimes the best thing you can do is spread your wings and fly. For you, you needed to experience a life that you couldn't have in Pleasureville. We all knew that, especially Aiden. That's why he didn't fight you when you left. But every once in a while, those wings carry you back to where you belong. Dreams change. Sometimes, love is right where you left it."

Her eyes, so warm and caring, are shining brightly as she stares up at me. Each word was like a lightning strike, a direct hit straight to my heart.

"Ready to go?" Aiden asks as he returns to the kitchen. I'm sure he can feel the shift in the room. The air feels emotionally charged, and no one speaks for several heart-pounding seconds.

Becky offers a friendly, knowing smile as she squeezes my hand once more. It's as if she can see the turmoil brewing deep in my gut. "You two enjoy the night," she says before turning her attention to the dishes in the sink.

Aiden holds the door open for me as we slip out the back. We make our way through Becky's flower garden as we head towards the largest of four horse barns. The garden looks better than I remember. Large Adirondack chairs and a two-person swing are positioned within the beautiful blooms in bright reds, oranges, yellows, and purples. I used to love coming over here and helping her weed the garden, soaking up every ounce of motherly time she would give me. When I left for New York, I didn't just leave Aiden. I left his parents, my parents, my brother, and friends too.

"Everything all right back there?" he asks as we approach the barn.

"Yeah. Your mom was just giving me one of her famous pep talks," I say with a small smile.

"Ahh, infamous insight from one Becky Hughes. I'm sure you've missed that." Aiden laughs, but it sounds hollow.

"I have. Missed it, I mean. I always loved spending time with your mom. She seemed to know just what to say to me, exactly when I needed to hear it."

"And did she this time? Say what you needed to hear?" His golden eyes are so clear as he stands before me, hand poised on the handle of the sliding door.

"I'm not sure yet," I answer honestly.

There are so many things to consider right now. I feel a bit like a boat lost at sea. I'm going through the motions, but I know that I can't continue to do it for much longer. Sooner or later, I'm going to have to sit down and really think about what I want. Not what my

A Place to Call Home

parents want. Not what Aiden wants. What *I* want. I did that once before and it took me a thousand miles away to New York City.

But suddenly, that dream isn't front and center in my mind. That dream is looking like something I see in the rearview mirror as opposed to something lying on the road ahead.

And that's the most confusing part of it all.

Is it just being here–in my hometown–with Aiden so close? Is that why my dream of being a famous wedding dress designer holds less appeal than it did just a few short weeks ago? Is it the hours I continually put in and the rabid boss I endure? The fact that I have few friends and less free time to enjoy them?

There is so much to consider, and right now, as I inhale Aiden's muskiness, along with the strong scent of horses, I'm left reeling.

"Come on," Aiden says as he grabs ahold of my hand and leads me into the massive barn. "I want you to meet my other girl."

* * *

As we approach the John Deere Gator parked beside the garage, I instantly know: I want to drive it. It's sitting there, beckoning me, with all of its green and yellow shininess. The bed of the UTV is filled with chopped wood and the keys are hanging from the ignition.

"What?" Aiden asks when he realizes I stopped a few feet back.

"I want to drive."

His eyes fill with surprise first, but it's quickly chased away with heat. Giving me that arrogant smile, he says, "I don't think so, Rainbow. This girl is brand new, and has too much power for you."

"I can handle whatever you throw at me, Aiden Hughes. This baby is begging to be driven," I say as I glide my hand over the sleek metal of the utility vehicle. I feel empowered as I watch his Adam's apple bob. "I have a feeling you just don't give her what she needs. And what she really needs is to be driven." And then, as I lean forward until I'm a mere breath away from his lips, I go in for the kill. "Hard."

Aiden gasps before his eyes narrow. "Get your cute ass in there before I spank it."

Now it's my turn to gasp.

Aiden walks around, slides into the passenger seat, and secures his seatbelt as if he didn't just threaten to mark my ass. As I slip in and do the same, he grabs the handle above his door and says, "Do your worst."

And just like that: the gauntlet has been thrown.

I start off a bit slow, getting a feel for the big utility vehicle, as I make my way around the barns and along the well-driven paths. As soon as we approach the pasture leading to Aiden's house, I stomp down on the pedal, throwing grass and leaving a trail of dust in my wake.

The UTV drives like a dream, and I'm having a blast as I make my way down the dirt driveway that I assume leads to Aiden's house. Since he doesn't direct me to take another route, I keep going.

When the timber breaks, I'm left reeling once more at the beautiful two-story log cabin situated perfectly within the clearing. A large front porch wraps from one end to the other, extending around the right side of the house towards the back. Aiden points to the carport attached to the garage, so I drive the vehicle around and park it.

"This place is stunning, Aiden," I tell him as I take in the spacious backyard.

"Come on, I'll show ya around," he says as he unbuckles both of our safety restraints.

Walking up the back porch, I hear the unmistakable barks of a dog. When Aiden opens the door without a key, I can't help but say, "Boy, you sure can't do that in New York."

Aiden chuckles. "I'm sure you can't."

Throwing open the back door, we're both greeted by a yellow lab with a wagging tail and floppy tongue. "Hey, boy. Meet my friend Colbi."

Instantly, I drop to my knees and receive a kiss from the big, hairy dog. "Oh my God, you are too cute!"

"Don't tell him that. I can barely live with his ego as it is," Aiden says as he throws on the kitchen light.

"What's his name?"

"Gus." As if to answer my question, the dog barks loudly and raises his paw to shake.

"Easy there, lady killer. If you're not careful, you'll pull a stitch," Aiden says to the friendly K-9.

"A stitch? Did something happen to him?" I ask, checking over the big fluff ball with my eyes and hands.

"He had his manhood stripped from him last week. He's still slow to get around so that's why I didn't take him up to Mom's with me. He also knows that's where I went which would be why he's giving me the stink-eye right now."

As if to confirm Aiden's claim, the dog glances up and gives him a wary look. "Don't worry, boy. Mom took care of you, too." Aiden pulls a baggy from his pocket and produces a strip of bacon, which Gus inhales in one quick bite.

"Can I get you something to drink?"

"What do you have?" I ask, taking in the spacious kitchen around me. The entire downstairs has an open floor plan. Just beyond the kitchen is a small dining room, which leads to the living room.

A Place to Call Home

"I have water, diet Dr. Pepper, and light beer. There's also a bit of milk, but I can't guarantee its freshness," he says while taking a sniff from the quart of milk.

"Diet Dr. Pepper? I thought you hated that stuff," I state, smiling over my shoulder.

"What can I say, it grew on me." Aiden always scoffed at my choice of beverage when we were dating.

"I'll have a beer," I finally say, turning and watching as he retrieves two cans of a light beer from his refrigerator. Aiden pops the top on the first one and hands it to me before doing the same for the second.

"Want that tour?"

I nod as he leads me towards the dining room where a small table sits with papers spread across the top. "Sorry, I was reviewing some notes on a few fillies we've got our eye on." He scoops up the papers into a single pile and sets them aside.

"I'm proud of you for stepping up and taking over operations when your dad died. I'm sure it wasn't easy," I tell him, coming up beside him.

His hazel eyes bore into me with so much intensity and appreciation, it almost knocks me for a loop. "Thank you. That means a lot to me, but it was an easy decision to make. Running this farm is the only thing I've ever really wanted to do."

I follow behind as Aiden leads me into the living room. A massive stone fireplace takes up the center wall. A plush brown couch and matching recliner sits in front of it. It's a beautifully warm and inviting room. I can almost imagine snuggling up on the couch in front of a blazing fire.

"Uh, where's the TV?" I ask after realizing there isn't one in the room.

"I don't have one."

"What? No TV? What do you do at night without one?"

"Actually, I'm rarely in here. I come here to eat and sleep, that's about it. Between four horse barns and watching for new foals through the winter, I'm only home long enough to grab a bite to eat before falling into bed."

"Don't you have help for that?"

"Yeah, but I only keep them on during the day and on weekends. We've got three high school kids that come out to muck stalls and help with the feeding and exercise. Another is a junior in college and plans to attend vet school, so she's been coming out the past couple of summers and helping out."

"Wow, no television, huh? Do you have running water or did I miss the outhouse out back? What about heat? Does that wood fireplace heat the whole house?" I ask, my voice laced with sarcasm.

A Place to Call Home

Aiden's laughter is music to my ears. "I have electricity, running water, and propane heat. Though, the fireplace does do wonders in the winter to help with the heating."

Glancing around, I notice the stairs nestled behind a massive bookshelf. Aiden was always a big reader. Science fiction and military non-fiction, mostly. So I'm not surprised in the least when I see several titles lining the shelves that fall into either genre.

"I saw this movie in the theatre. I bawled my eyes out."

"Yeah, books about Chris Kyle are some of my favorite. Your brother actually started me on that one," he says, pointing to a well-worn book with a torn cover. "That's Marcus' copy. He brought it over a couple of years back and left it here for me. Every time he was on leave, he'd sneak over and grab it to read. But I always found it returned to the shelf when he went back to his base."

"That sounds like him." The air becomes thick with tension. "I miss him like crazy," I whisper, staring at that worn paperback book.

"Me too. Come on, let's go upstairs," Aiden says, drawing a quizzical look from me. "Don't worry, I'm not going to take advantage of you." Together we walk towards the stairs. "Unless you want me to." Then he throws one of those cocky smirks over his shoulder at me and my insides melt. My legs are practically jelly-like as we climb upward, my face flush with embarrassment from his innuendo.

The upstairs consists of a master bedroom and a smaller one that Aiden uses as an office/workout room. Judging by the layer of dust on top of the desk, I'd say he rarely uses the office for its intent. The free weights and treadmill, on the other hand, appear well used and dust-free.

Through the master bedroom, Aiden opens a sliding glass door, which leads to a small deck with two chairs. My first thought is wondering who sits in the other chair beside him? I do my best to shake off the sudden feeling of jealousy, but it just won't leave. My brain latches onto the image of Aiden and some no-faced brunette enjoying quiet nights under the stars on this deck. Does she like to play his stargazing game with him? Does she ever see a rainbow in those stars?

"Have a seat," he says, shutting the door behind him, Gus lying on the floor on the opposite side of the door.

"You have a beautiful home. This deck is wonderful," I say as I look down at the backyard and surrounding timber.

"Thanks. This is my favorite place. I enjoy sitting out here and watching the stars. If I could get away with sitting here year round, I would. It's a place of solitude. Nothing but peace and quiet."

"You have two chairs. I'm sure it's not always quiet," I say. Open mouth, insert foot. The last thing I want to know more about is Aiden's dating life. I know it happens–he's confirmed it–but that doesn't mean I want to dwell on and talk about it.

"I never use both chairs. No one has ever been up here. Your brother and I always hang out on the deck below."

I glance over and meet his stormy eyes. They've suddenly taken on a molten, smoky appearance and my breath catches in my throat.

"Tell me about Marcus' trip to New York last winter?" Aiden asks, turning his attention to the beer can in his hand.

"Well, I knew Mom and Dad were coming for Christmas, but I wasn't expecting Marcus. He emailed me the week before and said he couldn't get away since they were preparing for deployment back to Afghanistan. When I opened the door and saw him standing there, I knocked him down in a tackle-hug."

"He was so damn excited to surprise you. He talked about it for weeks."

"I was completely blown away. Mom and Dad stayed at the hotel down the road that they always stay at, but I convinced Marcus to stay with me. I tried giving him my full-sized bed, but he wouldn't hear of it. He slept three nights on my old, uncomfortable couch and never once complained.

The memory of my six-foot-four brother sleeping on my five-foot couch brings a smile to my face. He could have easily stayed at the hotel with our parents and had a good night's sleep, but he didn't. He chose to stay with me, taking four-minute speed showers to ensure we each had enough hot water to get clean.

"Can I ask you something?"

"Sure."

"Why haven't you ever come home for Christmas? Why do you stay in New York by yourself? I'm sure your parents would have loved to have you with them on Christmas morning."

I exhale deeply. We're getting closer and closer to the invisible line I drew in the sand when I left Pleasureville for the Big Apple. "When I left for New York, I just wanted a clean break. I wanted to start over, fresh. I was determined to make something of myself and I was afraid that if I returned, someone would try to convince me not to go back."

"I don't recall anyone trying to convince you to not go in the first place, Rainbow."

"No, you're right. I could tell my parents were saddened by my decision but it was only because it was so far away. It had nothing to do with me wanting to spread my wings." Becky's words come back to me with force. "And you. You encouraged me to go."

"Is it because you were afraid someone would talk you out of it or because *you* were afraid you'd talk yourself out of it?" His question hangs heavily between us. An anvil of reason and logic ready to slice and dice at me.

I'm not ready to say the words, but I'm sure he can see them in my tearful eyes. Aiden is absolutely right. I was terrified that if I returned home, I'd give up and never return to New York. That I'd walk away from my dream and settle for a life in Pleasureville. I'd settle into a life with Aiden, and even though a life with him surely wouldn't be anything less than amazing, I was afraid. I was afraid that I'd lose myself–or worse yet, that I'd never even discover the real me. And then I'd resent him.

And that thought is unimaginable.

Aiden leans forward, sets his beer down on the deck, and reaches for my hands. "I'm very proud of you, sweetheart. I only ever wanted you to live the life you wanted and be happy. If that happiness took you a thousand miles away, then that's what I wanted. As hard as it was to let you go, I knew then that it was for the best."

As a tear slips down my cheek, I whisper, "Thank you. It means a lot to hear you say that."

"I should have said it a long time ago, but I'll admit that I was still a little upset. Not at you, but at the situation. I was heartbroken and sad for a long time after you left. I missed you like crazy. I went from having one of my best friends with me all the time to not having her in my life at all. It was a big adjustment for me."

"I never meant to hurt you, Aiden."

"I know that, Rainbow. And I never meant to hurt you either. I loved you more than life itself, and if letting you go was what you needed, then it was what I had to do."

The tears fall in earnest down my face. So many years of pent-up emotions and unsaid words finally spill from my eyes. "I missed you so much." I choke on the words, almost unable to get them out.

Aiden moves quickly, squatting between my legs. He pulls me into a fierce hug, letting my tears soak into his navy blue shirt. "I missed you every moment of every day. I still miss you."

Using the pad of his thumb, Aiden catches a few of my falling tears. His eyes hold so much sadness–sadness for the love we once shared and then lost. But also in those hazel eyes, I see desire. Sparks of heat begin to replace the sadness until there's nothing left but an inferno of raging lust and yearning.

My breathing is ragged as Aiden leans in. His lips seem bashful at first, but turn ravenous quickly as he takes me in a bruising kiss. There's nothing sweet in this kiss. No, it's firm and devouring as his tongue slips between his lips and glides along the seam of my mouth.

As soon as I part my mouth, he overtakes me. His tongue plunders and plunges, leaving me breathless and wanton. I grip his neck, fearful that he'll pull away or slow down the kiss. Slowing down is the last thing I want right now. I want to forget. I want to feel. I want to be worshipped in a way that only Aiden can provide.

Only him.

I move forward until my ass is barely sitting on the chair and I connect with his midsection. Tugging his t-shirt until it's pulled from his jeans, my hands connect with his taut abs. The hard, unforgiving muscles that can only come from years of manual labor and hard work, jump beneath my touch. His skin is hot, scorching my fingers as I explore the man he's become.

"I want to touch you so fucking bad," Aiden groans between kisses he places on my chin and neck.

"Then touch me, Aiden." His golden eyes meet mine as if seeking confirmation. I see his passion and desire for me laced in those beautiful eyes. "Please. Touch me."

Aiden reaches down and grabs the hem of my shirt and pulls it over my head. The cool night air chills my exposed skin, causing goose bumps. My nipples pebble through my pink lace bra and seem to draw his attention.

He dips his head down and takes one lace-covered bud between his lips. I can't stop the moan that erupts from somewhere deep in my throat. His mouth is like a direct line straight to my core. My entire body is alive and yearning for this man and his magical mouth. He's the *only* man to ever make me feel this way.

I continue to stroke the planes of his chest beneath his shirt as he devours my chest with his lips. Giving the material a push, he finally removes his shirt. *And holy hell.* I could tell Aiden was cut, but seeing him without a shirt, the ripped muscles and that sexy V dropping into the top of his Wranglers, leaves me speechless. I summon up every bit of my restraint to keep from humping his leg like a dog.

Without saying a word, Aiden unsnaps my shorts. I lift my hips, never once taking my eyes off him. He's devouring me with every inch of flesh he exposes. His eyes are primal and raw as he takes in my little scrap of pink lace panties. There's nothing sexier than slipping on a pair of scandalous panties then seeing the reaction to said panties through the eyes of the man you crave.

"Jesus, Colbi, I've died and gone to heaven," he says as he runs his hands slowly up my thighs.

Reaching up, I wrap my arms around his neck. "Well, not yet, you haven't."

I pull him forward until our mouths are together again. Our tongues duel in the most erotic way, lips nipping and sucking at each other until neither of us can take it any longer. Reaching forward, I pull the button of his jeans, my hands anxiously dropping the zipper and diving beneath the coarse denim.

Aiden stands up quickly, pulling my hands free from his pants before I can cop a feel on the goods. In one quick well-rehearsed move, Aiden pushes his pants down. Fortunately, his boots are slip-ons so it only takes him a second to lose them and his jeans. When he stands up, he's wearing a pair of sexy black boxer briefs and sporting the biggest erection I've ever seen. Oh yes, time has been very good to Aiden Hughes.

I inhale sharply at his thick, hard cock. My mouth salivates to taste and my fingers tingle to touch him. As I reach forward, however, Aiden swats my hand away. "Not yet, sweetheart. I won't be able to withstand one touch from you before I explode, and I'm not lookin' to embarrass myself."

Instead, Aiden returns his attention to the junction of my legs. His deft fingers glide over the lace panties, which, to my mortification, I realize are practically dripping wet. Moving the material aside, Aiden exposes my throbbing core. The cool air against the heated flesh is sweet torture as he lowers his head to the apex of my thighs.

The first swipe of his hot tongue almost does me in. Aiden lays his hand across my stomach to keep me from jackknifing off the chair further. His mouth devours my core, licking and sucking at my swollen nub as if it were the best tasting lollipop he's ever experienced.

I should be embarrassed at how quickly Aiden brings me to orgasm. With a few fixed swipes of his tongue, I'm flying over the ledge and diving headfirst into total oblivion. "More," he says firmly without lifting his mouth from my wet flesh.

Before I can even formulate a response, Aiden slides two fingers into my body and curls them upward, deep inside of me. His mouth latches onto my pulsating clit again and, once more, I see stars. I didn't even know it was possible to orgasm back to back so quickly, but apparently it's very possible. Aiden makes it possible.

Practically lying atop the wooden chair, I find myself completely spent, unable to move. My eyelids are heavy, but the sound of Aiden's movement causes me to open them. And what a show I am treated to! Aiden is sliding the briefs down his powerful legs, dropping them onto the deck with the rest of our clothes. His erection jets straight out from his body, large and very proud.

And just like that, I'm suddenly wide-awake.

Aiden grabs his jeans and removes a foil packet from his wallet. When he returns his attention to me, it's to devour my body once more with his eyes. It's as if he can't look his fill of me.

Kneeling before me, Aiden unsnaps the plastic clasp of my bra, freeing my breasts from their lacy restraints. He also wastes no time getting rid of my panties. Rolling on the condom, he looks up at me once more. "Are you sure?"

"Very sure," I tell him before his erection connects with my sensitive core.

"Don't close your eyes," he tells me as he lines his body up with mine.

As Aiden slowly pushes inside of me, it's like coming home. The tightness and fullness of it fades away, leaving only my love for him. And I do. I love him. I know I do. I never stopped.

"Are you okay?" he whispers hoarsely, stopping when he's halfway seated inside of me.

"I'm more than okay," I confirm, wiggling my hips, encouraging him to continue.

Aiden pulls out slightly before pushing forward again. This Aiden is so much bigger than I remember, and I start to wonder if I'll ever be able to take him all the way in.

"Relax, Rainbow," he tells me as he gently pushes further in.

When he's fully seated, I revel in the amazing fullness and eroticism of this moment. My breathing is harsh and jaded, and my body has thundered back to life in a tsunami of desire. How I could possibly want this man so fiercely after two amazing orgasms is beyond me.

"I gotta move, sweetheart," Aiden says through ragged breath, sweat starting to break out on his brow.

"Then move."

And holy shit, does he move. His strokes are long and deliberate as he moves his body within mine. He gently holds my legs, wrapping those long fingers around the outsides of my thighs. Aiden claims my body with his own, carefully driving me towards the finish line.

The closer I get, so does Aiden. His hips begin to move in a hurried, crazed sort of way, as if he can't control his body's need for release any further. The primal look in his eyes is my undoing. I grab his neck and pull him down, consuming his mouth in a blazing kiss, as he continues to pound into me. The friction of his body against my swollen clit sends me headlong into another, less intense, yet equally satisfying orgasm. "God, yes…" I groan, his name the only other word on my lips.

My internal muscles grip his shaft, pulling him tightly and triggering his own release. Our eyes remain open and locked on each other, our lips barely a whisper apart, and our moans of release filling the quiet night.

When the aftershocks of pleasure start to subside, Aiden places soft, sweet kisses on my swollen lips. Our breath mixes in short, labored pants and our bodies molding together from sweat. I could die right now and I'd go a happy woman. Being here, wrapped in Aiden's arms, naked from amazing sex, is heaven.

And I don't want to think about it ending. Again.

"Don't do that. Don't think about it," he whispers. Aiden always had the ability to know exactly what I was thinking, sometimes even before I knew. It was part of the reason why we clicked so well together.

I can't deny that I wasn't thinking it, so I don't. Keeping my arms firmly locked around his neck, Aiden lifts me, holding me tightly against his body. I realize as he walks me into his bedroom, over his sleeping dog, that he's still completely seated inside of me. And that he's unmistakably hard once more. The realization is both exhilarating and intimidating.

As Aiden starts to set me down on the bed, I latch onto him, not wanting to lose his body from within mine. "I need to grab you a washcloth," he says, trying to move, but unable to eradicate his cock from my core.

"I need you to move," I tell him boldly, working my internal muscles against him.

His groan fills the room. "Sweetheart, you're going to be sore tomorrow if we do this again."

"I need you, Aiden. Please," I beg him, looking deep into those stunning golden eyes.

Never one to be able to refuse me, Aiden reaches over and grabs a fresh condom out of his bedside table. I let him pull free only long enough to sheath himself once more before I push his shoulder, sending him sprawling on the comforter.

Climbing on his body, I slowly kiss my way down his chest, licking and sucking on his nipples. I grind myself against his thick erection, coating his cock in my wetness, until his cock surges upward, filling me in one swift, fluid motion.

We both sigh in complete contentment, our bodies uniting again in a moment of pure bliss. I move up and down, riding him like a cowgirl at a rodeo until we're both left satisfied and exhausted. And then I curl up into him, his warm body tucked protectively around mine.

I don't know what the morning will bring or the next day or the next. But I do know that I'm completely happy right here, right now. I'm elated to be with Aiden, falling asleep in his arms. Wrapped up in the only man I've ever loved.

I'm finally at peace.

Chapter Six

Aiden

Sunshine blinding me through the windows is a rare occurrence. I'm usually up well before the sun, enjoying my second cup of coffee as I prepare for my day. It's been a long damn time since I woke up with my arms wrapped around lush curves and soft skin. And an even longer time since that woman was Colbi Leigh.

My mind instantly returns to the night I spent with her. First, on the deck outside, then the two times we made love in this bed. A bed that has only ever held myself. Alone. Her scent of jasmine fills my being with familiarity and hope. Hope that maybe this won't be the last time I wake with her in my arms.

But then reality starts to set in. I know she's only here for another week, and then she returns to her life in New York. A life that doesn't include me.

Knowing that Colbi didn't return to Pleasureville but a few times in her eight-year absence because of her fears, still heckles me. I let her go so she could follow her dreams. I never would have pressured her to stay with me during any of her return visits. She knows that, and now I know that she wasn't worried about me convincing her to stay: she was worried about her own convictions.

So as I snuggle against the woman of my dreams, her back to my front, I grasp onto that little sliver of hope. That maybe, someday, Colbi will return to Pleasureville and to me. Chances are I'm still going to be left heartbroken and alone when she leaves in a week, but at least I know it's not anything I can't handle. She left before and I survived. I'll survive this time, too.

Colbi wriggles her perfect ass against my dick, causing my morning wood to surge to life. "Vixen, you better watch it, or you're going to find yourself flat on your back with my dick buried inside of you again," I whisper heatedly in her ear as I move her until she's beneath me, grabbing two handfuls of that lush ass.

"That doesn't sound like much of a threat," she sasses, my dick rigid and raring to go once more as I rub it against her slick pussy.

"If you want to be able to walk today, I suggest you keep it PG. I have no problem keeping you here, bending to my every whim for the rest of the day."

"See, I still don't see the threat. That sounds like a great day to me," she says, wiggling against my cock once more. She's two seconds away from being ravished.

"Unfortunately, I'm late for work. I should've been up at the barn a half hour ago," I say as I playfully bite her shoulder. Her gasp goes straight to my throbbing dick. I'm going to need a long, cold shower before I'll be able to function today.

As if reading my mind, Colbi says, "Well, forgive me for causing you to be late, but you do need to shower before you go, correct? And I need to shower." The look she gives me is down right scandalous. "See where I'm going with this, slugger?"

"Oh, I know exactly where you're going with this," I say moments before I stand up and throw her over my shoulder, carting her naked ass off towards the bathroom. "And I know exactly what you're going to get when we get there," I add, playfully slapping her ass as I step into the adjoining bathroom.

* * *

Three. That's how many nights I've spent meeting Colbi down at the pond to enjoy stargazing before we find ourselves tangled up together in my bed. We instantly fell into a comfortable routine that involves plenty of laughs, talks, and sex.

As that ominous deadline draws closer, I find myself more agitated and restless than ever. It's Thursday night and I'm anxious to see her. As I do every other night, I sense her presence before she makes herself known.

"Tell me about your job," I say, pulling her tightly against me. I feel her tense instantly. "We've been skirting around it the entire time you've been here, but I want to know. I need to know about that part of your life."

Colbi sighs deeply. "My senior year, I was chosen for an elite internship with one of the top designers in New York. I was ecstatic and couldn't wait to finally get some real experience under my belt. My first day with Alana Kensington, I knew I was doing what I always wanted to do. And at the end of the internship, a position opened up. She offered me a job as her assistant."

"That's amazing, Colbi."

"I guess. I mean, I was excited and all, but something was missing."

"What?"

"Designing. I am basically her gopher. She has me running copies, making calls, and getting her coffee, but I have yet to work on a real wedding dress with her. I basically hold the pins while she works the material into the bride's dream dress. I tried to show her some of my designs on several occasions, but she brushes me off like I'm not worth her time. To this day, she has yet to look at any of the drawings I've offered. I've been very explicitly reminded, on more than one occasion, that I work for her. That my designs have no place in her company."

A Place to Call Home

"Quit. She clearly doesn't know talent when she sees it."

"I can't just quit, Aiden. Alana Kensington is an amazing resource and a true trendsetter in the business."

"But how is she any resource of yours if all you're doing is fetching her coffee or ordering her lunch? If you want to make it in that industry, you need to be known in the industry. You need to show your designs and work firsthand on dresses. If she won't look at your ideas, find someone who will," I tell her, my words full of passion. It sickens me that she's spent all this time in New York only to never reach the dreams she set out to achieve.

"You make it sound so easy," she whispers.

"It can be that easy. If Alana doesn't want to see your brilliance, then find someone who will. Go door to door if you have to. Knock on the door of every custom wedding designer in New York until someone recognizes your talent and begs you to work with them."

Her laughter casts off the water. "You have so much faith in me and you haven't even seen my work. I could suck."

"There's no way you suck. You wouldn't have received that fancy shmancy internship with that high flutin' woman if you sucked."

"If you say so," she chuckles.

"I say so," I say, running my hand over her bare shoulder. "Will you show me sometime? Your drawings and stuff?"

"Okay. If you really want to see them," she says, gazing up at me. Those big blue eyes filled with so much wonder and excitement.

"I want to. And I want you to seriously think about finding another place to work. I'm not trying to bully you or anything, but if you're not doin' what you've always dreamed about doin', well, then it's time to find someplace where you can do it."

We're both quiet for quite some time afterwards. It bothers me that she went off to New York to do her thing, only to have some bitch from hell boss hold her back. The concept makes my blood boil and my pulse race. I know it wasn't going to be easy for her–no dream worth having is easy–but it seems like any real role model would be more interested in teaching than hindering. My gut tells me that her boss is holding her back, and I don't like it.

Not one bit.

Later that night, while we're nestled together, naked, beneath a blanket on the floor in front of the roaring fireplace, I fixate on the fact that we're down to a few nights. Colbi fell asleep hours ago, but I haven't found the ability to close my eyes. It's well after midnight now, the date officially Friday. And Colbi leaves on Sunday. She leaves in just two short days.

Our time is coming to an end, and as exhaustion finally starts to take hold, I grab on to every ounce of strength I possess, every bit of fortitude I can find. Because when it's all said and done, I'm going to need that strength, that fortitude, to get up and keep going come Monday morning. The morning after she leaves again. When I wake up alone.

* * *

"What are you doing here so late?" Mom asks as I slip into her kitchen to find her sitting at the table, head engrossed in a crossword puzzle. Even though it's Friday night, I knew exactly where I'd find her.

"I was getting ready to head to the house and thought I'd check to see if you had any manicotti left."

Mom gives me a warm smile before she gets up to retrieve a plastic container of cheese-stuffed noodles. "Sit down and let me fix you some."

"You don't have to do that. I'm a big boy," I remind her as I take the opposite seat to the one she vacated.

"I know you are, but a mother never minds waiting on her son."

I laugh, incredulously. "If I recall correctly, you constantly reminded me when I was younger that you weren't put on this earth to wait on me hand and foot."

Mom waves off my statement. "That was when you were a boy and I was teaching you how to be self-sufficient. Now that you know, I don't mind helping." She places three large noodles on a plate, covers them with sauce, and places it in the microwave. "Why aren't you with Colbi tonight?"

"She went to dinner with her parents, and then she was going to help them plan a Memorial Day gathering on Monday at Marcus's grave."

"Scott mentioned that she's not staying for the service on Monday," Mom says as she retrieves the plate from the microwave and places it in front of me.

"No, she has to be to work on Monday morning, so her flight leaves Sunday." The thought causes the bite I just ate to turn to lead in my gut. Just the thought of her leaving on Sunday and possibly never returning again is enough to do me in.

"What are you going to do about telling that girl that you're still in love with her?" she says as she sits down across from me.

"Wow, Mom, don't hold back any. And who says I'm still in love with her?"

"Oh, please, boy. I've been watching you two for the past week. You love her the same as you did before

A Place to Call Home

she left. In fact, I'd bet money on the fact that you never stopped. Am I right?"

I just look at her, refusing to give the answer she's rooting for. But I also know she doesn't need my confirmation to know it's true. "Whether I'm in love with Colbi or not doesn't matter. She's leaving the day after tomorrow to fly home."

"You could ask her to stay," Mom gently prods.

I set my fork down, all thoughts of food abandoned the moment Mom started talking about love and Colbi. "I won't do that. I won't ask her to stay. Not for me, Mom. She has to want to stay for herself. Otherwise, it'll never work. She'll be miserable and I can't stand the thought of that. I'd rather have her happy in New York City than sad here with me."

"Maybe she won't be miserable here, Aiden. Maybe she needs to be reminded of what is here waiting for her."

"You don't think I haven't wanted to get down on my knees and beg her to stay? You don't think that the thought of her getting on that plane isn't tearing me up inside? The thought of never holding her again or kissing her? It *kills* me to think about it, but I won't ask her to stay, Mom. I won't be the reason she's unhappy."

"What makes you think she would be unhappy?"

"I don't know, but I do know that she would always wonder 'what if.' I want her to stay because she loves me. I want her to stay because she can't live without me. I want her to stay because it's the only place she belongs. But I want her to come to that realization on her own. I won't encourage or sway her either way. I will support whatever decision she makes."

"Even if that decision takes her back to New York?"

I swallow hard before I answer. "Yes."

Because at the end of the day, I will let her go. I will let her go the same way I let her go eight years ago. And this time, when she boards that plane, she'll take what's left of my heart with her.

Chapter Seven

Colbi

"You're sure we can't talk you into staying until after the service on Monday? It's Memorial Day." Mom has asked this question no less than four times since our evening began with dinner at the café a few hours ago.

"I can't, Mom. Alana has been very lenient these past few days, but I think her patience is wearing thin. She called me, again, this morning to confirm my return for Monday."

"But, your brother passed away, for God's sake. I would think she could grant you one extra day to be with your family. Who makes their employees work on Memorial Day, anyway?" Her words are like daggers straight to my chest. I want to be here with my parents on Monday to honor and celebrate Marcus' life, but Alana made it very clear on the phone this morning: be in the office at eight o'clock Monday morning or find a new job.

"She can't stay, Karen. Quit badgering the poor girl," my dad says from his seat across from me. "I'm just glad she's here with us now." Dad's smile is warm and genuine as he winks over his glass of sweet tea.

"I know. I just hate the thought of her returning to New York. It's so far away," she says, her eyes misting with unshed tears.

"What if I don't return to New York?" I ask, the words flying from my lips before I have a chance to reel them back or consider their meaning.

Two pairs of shocked eyes stare back at me. Calling upon every bit of courage I possess, I continue. "I mean, what if my dream has changed a little bit? What if I decide that being a big-wig wedding dress designer in New York City isn't what I want anymore?"

"What is it that you want?" my dad asks.

"Maybe something a little closer to home." I look over their heads and fixate on the wall. Memories of our conversations at the pond, dinner at Aiden's house, and making love in his bed flood my thoughts. "Maybe something with a little house in the country and a husband and dog. And maybe someday a few kids to chase around my parents' yard."

Suddenly, that picture sounds perfect. That image is bloody perfect. Like a dream.

My dream.

"You want to come home?" Mom asks, each word filled with more hope than the last.

"I think so."

Dad gives me a pointed look. "You think? You need to be sure, baby girl. I want you to be happy, and I

A Place to Call Home

won't settle for anything less. I take it you're talking about Aiden?" I give a quick nod. "And you want to come home and be with him? You'd be fine leaving everything in New York and coming back to Pleasureville?"

"Yes," I tell him, that one word flying from my lips without any hesitation.

"Then, I guess I only have one more question." I stare up at my dad, wide-eyed and filled with excitement. "How soon can we get your stuff back home?"

I laugh hard before jumping up and throwing my arms around his neck. My mom silently cries from her seat at the table until I embrace her in a massive hug. "Can you guys do me a favor?" I ask, though my own tears.

"Anything," Mom sniffles.

"Let's keep this between us for the time being. I have some things to do in New York before I make this official. But then, I'll be home. Promise."

Chapter Eight

Aiden

Sunday. D-Day.

Colbi hugs her parents on the front porch while I load her new black suitcase in my truck. There was no way in hell I was letting her leave with that old, beat-up broken piece of shit she arrived with, so I stopped by a supercenter thirty-minutes away on my way home the other night.

I'm honestly a little surprised by the lack of tears I see up on that porch. I would have thought for sure that Karen would be bawling her eyes out. Hell, it's taking everything I have not to bawl *my* eyes out.

After final hugs and promises to visit soon are exchanged, Colbi makes her way towards my truck. I'm on autopilot as I help her inside the cab, shut the door, and walk around to the driver's side. With a quick wave to her parents, I pull out of the driveway and head towards Louisville.

A few minutes into the drive, Colbi reaches over and grabs my hand, locking her fingers with mine. No words are said the entire fifty-minute trip, but I'm certain none are needed. What could either of us possibly say at this point?

When I pull up to the airport departures, I stop the truck at the curb. I opt to drop her at the terminals, not looking to draw out the goodbye any longer than necessary. Why torture ourselves more than we need to, right? She's leaving, plain and simple. End of story.

"Thank you for everything," she says, stepping up on the curb. I deposit the suitcase at her feet, and stuff my hands in my pockets.

"You're welcome." Lame.

Colbi reaches for me, wrapping her long arms around my neck, and pulls me into her. I go willingly into her embrace. "I'm going to miss you, Aiden."

"I'm going to miss you, too," I reply, hugging her with everything I have, wishing that the tighter I hug, the despair I feel would somehow squeeze from my body.

"I'll see you soon," she says, turning those tear-filled, crystal blue eyes on me. Those damn tears cut me to the quick, like a knife straight to the heart.

I nod my reply, unable to formulate words. It saddens me that it'll probably be another eight years before I see her again.

As she bends down to grab her suitcase, I long to say those three little words that are teetering on the tip of my tongue. Three words that I haven't said in so fucking long. Three words that are only for her.

But I know it wouldn't change her leaving, so I bite my tongue and don't say them.

Before she turns to go, Colbi leans forward on her tiptoes and brushes her lips against mine. The kiss is soft and nothing like the one I'd prefer, but I know it's right for the moment. It's a kiss of goodbye. So, I return her tender kiss, holding back the feelings I long to unleash on her.

The kiss ends all too soon, and she turns towards the terminal. As she steps through the sliding door, Colbi turns back to face me with a smile. "Aiden, I'll see you soon."

Her parting words stay with me long after she walks through the doorway, long after my drive back to Pleasureville, and long after I tuck myself into the bed that still smells like her. I toss and turn for the better part of the night, unable to find a comfortable position or calm the erratic beat of my heart.

My mind replays every moment we've shared over the last two weeks. From finding her distraught and crying in the airport to making love to her repeatedly under the stars last night, our time together has proven to be, once again, too fucking short.

What did she mean when she said she'd see me soon? Is she already planning a return visit? I highly doubt it. Not with the boss she has. But maybe she'll not stay away so damn long the next time. Maybe I really will see her soon. Anything is better than eight years.

My heart bleeds as it registers her loss. The ache in my chest isn't going away any time soon. I'm left with a void, a place where my heart used to be, because fuck knows my heart flew a thousand miles away and is sleeping in New York City.

My heart is gone.

And I'm left alone. Again.

* * *

Four weeks. That's how long it's been since Colbi left, taking a big piece of me with her. I've received a few random text messages over the course of the month, but that's nothing compared to seeing her, touching her. Sure, I've thought about going after her. I've pictured a happy reunion as she opens the door and finds me standing there. I've imagined exactly what I'd say to convince her to return to Pleasureville with me. I've dreamed about that actually happening.

But, I won't. As miserable as I might be, her happiness is what really matters.

Scott left a few days ago to visit friends. It's odd to me that he left Karen at home, alone, so close to the death of their son. But neither of them seemed worried about their four-day hiatus. Hell, even my mom doesn't seem concerned about the fact that Scott up and left.

He asked me to check on his wife every now and again, just to make sure she doesn't have any troubles at the house. While I'm there, I've found myself sitting and talking with her for hours before finally dragging myself home and falling into bed, exhausted but unable to sleep. I'm like the walking dead these past few weeks, and, unfortunately, there's no end in sight. Nothing short of having my arms wrapped around Colbi will alleviate the void in my chest.

The mid-June sun is intense as it beats down on me. After returning a feisty young colt to his stall, I remove my worn ball cap and pull the shirt over my head, wiping my forehead and chest with the drenched material. It's the second t-shirt I've soaked through already and it's only three o'clock; proof that it's going to be a bitch of a summer in Kentucky.

I make my way over to the hose and bend over, letting the cool water run over my head. When I stand back up, a distant honking fills the barn. Afraid that something is wrong with Mom, I take off at a hurried pace out the large door and notice a large U-Haul stopping in the middle of the lane.

As the dust starts to settle, the passenger door flies open and the most beautiful sight greets me. Colbi slides out of the truck cab and makes a beeline straight for me.

I'm rooted in place, transfixed by the wide smile spread across her face. I barely have enough time to get my wits together before she launches herself into my arms. It takes a couple of steps back until I'm able to right myself as she wraps both her arms and legs around me. The fact that she almost knocked my ass to the ground is a memory, the moment I have her in my arms. I enfold them firmly around her midsection, squeezing the ever-loving shit out of her.

"What in the hell are you doing here?" I say into her long blond hair, refusing to release the hold even for a second.

"I told you I would see you soon," she giggles. My heart is practically pulling a Hulk right now, trying to rip and tear its way through my chest.

"I don't understand. What are you doing here?" I ask, letting her body slide painfully slow down mine. Colbi seems preoccupied and it only takes a second for me to realize she's staring at my shirtless chest. "My eyes are up here," I tease with a huge wolfish grin.

"I know they are, but your chest is looking rather fine," she sasses, drinking her fill of the muscles on display.

"Do I need to get a shirt so we can continue this conversation?"

"It's not my fault you're such a distraction. Anyway, what were you saying?" she asks, returning those amazing blue eyes back up to my face.

"Here. What are you doing here, Colbi?"

"Well, I realized something when I was home a month ago. I wasn't really happy in New York City anymore."

I force myself to take a deep breath. Then a second. I'm practically tap dancing in the dirt and she's barely started to talk. "You weren't?"

"No," she says, shaking her head in confirmation. "I haven't been happy in a long time, and do you know why?"

Now it's my turn to shake my head. I can't seem to form words over the golf ball lodged in my throat.

"I wasn't happy because you weren't there. I didn't have you, Aiden. It didn't matter what I did, I still wasn't happy."

"But, what about your dream? What about designing wedding dresses and all that fancy stuff?" I ask, doing my best to keep the hope tamped down. But it's a losing battle as anticipation bubbles to the surface.

"Funny thing about dreams is they're not really complete without the one you love. Turns out, there are dress designers all over the U.S. willing to take a chance on a young apprentice and give them a shot at following their dreams."

Colbi seems to take a deep breath, channeling her inner calm, before she continues. "Did you know there's a fabulous dress shop in Louisville? The owner, Mrs. Nicholson, has a very interesting story. She has been looking for someone to bring into the business for a year now. Someone looking for more than just a nine to five. Her daughter was planning to take over, but as an inspiring dress designer herself, she was offered a position with Royalty Designs five years ago, and she couldn't refuse it. This left poor Mrs. Nicholson in need of someone to buy her out of the business she built from the ground up just out of college in 1972.

"Well, I met with Mrs. Nicholson yesterday and she offered me a position within her boutique, Timeless Dresses. And not just any position, but one where I'll learn all I need to know about running the day-to-day of a wedding and formal dress boutique. At the end of the first year, I have the option to purchase. I start next Monday."

I realize I'm holding my breath as I listen to her spell out her plans–her future. Forcing myself to take a deep breath, I focus on the smile spreading across those pink lips. "Jesus, Colbi, that's freaking amazing," I tell her, pulling her into a tight hug.

"That's not all of it," she mumbles, her face presses tightly against my neck.

"There's more?" I ask, chuckling.

"The daughter who works for Royalty Designs? Turns out she was visiting her mom yesterday so I met her as well. We got to chitchatting and she asked to look at some of my designs. Turns out, they've been talking about adding designers to the Royalty family. She made a call to her boss, and the next thing I knew, I'm on a conference call with the head of design for Royalty, Rosalie Dranger. Jenna Nicholson sent some of my designs to Rosalie via text when we were talking. They offered me a pay-per-design contract right then and there. Can you believe it? They want to buy some of my designs! My designs could be in dress shops all over the world!" Colbi practically screams with excitement.

"I knew you could do it," I tell her, spinning her around until we're both dizzy. "So, you're moving to Louisville?" I ask, my heart thumping loudly in my chest.

Louisville isn't ideal, but it's a hell of a lot better than New York City. An hour trip is a hell of a lot more doable than an airplane ride. And, for Colbi, I'll drive as much as I need to see her. Having her here right now, at this exact moment, makes me realize I'll do whatever in the fuck it takes to be with her. I crave her. She is the air I breathe.

"Actually, I was talkin' to my Dad," she starts, looking over her shoulder to the man I consider my second father. Scott is resting his back casually against the cab of the large U-Haul truck doing everything he can *not* to look like he's eavesdropping on our conversation. "And I think I want to stay around here. It's not that bad of a commute every day."

"So, you want to stay here? In Pleasureville?" I try to mask the hopefulness and eagerness in my voice, but I can't. I pray she's about to say what I think she's going to say.

"Yeah, I want to stay here. In fact, I thought maybe I could stay right here. With you," she says, her voice all but a whisper, as those crystal blue eyes sparkle up at me like brilliant diamonds.

"Are you askin' if you can shack up with me?" I ask, the corner of my lip curving upward into a cocky grin.

"Only if you want me to." Her hushed words wash over me like rain. Fuck yes, I want her to move in with me.

Reaching forward, I pull her back into my arms. She fits against me perfectly, like puzzle pieces aligning to reveal the most glorious picture. "I'm still not gettin' a TV," I say, deadpanned.

"Oh, well then never mind. If there's no TV, then I'm out. I guess I'll just see if Dad will let me have my old room back," she sasses as she starts to turn in the direction of her dad.

Grasping her wrist gently before she can get away, I turn her back to face me. The smile I'm greeted with warms me clear down to my boots. "I guess we'll just have to work out a compromise then. Maybe we can figure out some way to keep us both entertained in the evenings…without a TV." I slide my fingers into her soft hair, which has always been like a direct line straight to my dick. In fact, it takes about 2.5 seconds before my pants are unbearably tight, my dick strains against the coarse material.

"I like the sound of that."

Her words fill me with elation as I firmly press my lips against hers, reveling in the feel of her softness against me. My mind races as visions of happily ever afters swirl around at neck breaking speed. When her tongue slips out and slides against the crease of my lips, all thought evaporates. It's just us: Colbi and me.

"Move in with me. Stay with me," I whisper without fully removing my lips from hers.

"Wherever you are, that's where I want to be. You are my home."

I devour her in a deep kiss. A kiss that promises her a future and cements my love for her. A kiss that can only lead to more passionate kisses and things that involve way less clothes.

A kiss of forever.

Epilogue

Colbi

"What do you think of those?" Aiden asks, pointing straight up. We're lying on the blanket, his hot skin against mine. The July night is humid, causing us each to lose most of our clothing as we stargaze in the clear night sky. Of course, to be honest, we lost those items of clothes when we decided to do a little skinny-dipping in the pond, long before the stargazing commenced.

"That's a marshmallow riding a pony," I tell him with a straight face.

Aiden's laughter fills the night and sends euphoria tingling through my body. "I don't even want to know why a marshmallow would be riding a pony, crazy girl."

"I think the question is why *wouldn't* a marshmallow be riding a pony, silly boy."

I've been home a month now and have settled into my new life in Pleasureville. The daily commute to Louisville is exciting and refreshing as I make my way towards the small dress boutique I could one day own. The prospect is exhilarating and fills me with hope.

It doesn't hurt either that I come home to Aiden every night. Even with his busy schedule of running the ranch, we always find time to come together at the end of the day. Often we eat together, followed by me assisting him with any remaining chores around the ranch. I've found plenty of time and inspiration to work on my gown designs for Royalty. In fact, I've sold four designs, and they plan to include them in their line next spring.

"What about that one?" Aiden asks, his voice with a bit of a hitch, as he fidgets beside me.

"That's a rhinoceros."

"No way, Rainbow. That doesn't look anything like a rhino. You need your eyes checked," he says, straight-faced.

"Well, excuse me, Mr. Stargazer Expert. What do *you* think it is?" I ask dramatically.

"I think it looks like an engagement ring."

It takes several moments before his words permeate the fog in my brain. *Did he just say…?*

Aiden rolls over to face me, and right there between his thumb and pointer finger, he holds a simple solitaire diamond ring. I gasp in shock, my eyes bouncing back and forth between his and the amazing ring.

"I knew the moment I saw you when you were ten-years-old that I was going to make you mine. I'm pretty sure I even said as much to Marcus when we were playing baseball. The bastard punched me in the gut. Told me if I ever hurt you, he'd do worse." Aiden chuckles a bit, lost for a second in the memory of an unforgettable moment with his oldest and dearest friend, my brother, may he rest in peace.

"We've wasted eight years, and I refuse to waste any more, Colbi. I love you. I've always loved you. I know, without a shadow of doubt that you were put on this earth for me, and I promise to spend the rest of my days proving to you that we were made to be together. Marry me. Spend the rest of your life with me."

Aiden stares over at me, not moving a muscle; apparently not even breathing. He looks to be holding his breath as he waits for me to say something. It's not lost on me that we're both laying here in this place. Here, at the pond between his house and mine, where we would come together as friends and lovers in our youth, is where he's asking me to spend the rest of my life with him.

My heart threatens to explode from my chest as I take in the man I love more than life itself. His hair is wild as it dries in the night air. A day's worth of dark stubble dusts his firm jaw. His neck works overtime to swallow. But it's his eyes where I see everything I need to know. I see his love and adoration for me. I see his trust and his excitement. I see my future.

So I give him the only answer I can. "Yes."

Aiden lets out a loud whoop as he sits up, pulling me with him. On my knees across from him, he slides the most beautiful diamond onto my ring finger. It's a perfect fit: just like him.

"I love you so much, Rainbow," he chokes out before leaning forward and pulls my lips towards his. His tongue savors and tastes me as we seal our declaration in a heated kiss.

"I love you, too." Four little words that represent everything I am and everything I feel for this man. Because he is my everything. My reason for living. My life.

Chuckling against my lips, I pull back and look bemused at my fiancé. "What's so funny?" I ask.

"Your brother. You know, after I told him I was going to marry you someday, he said something that always stuck with me. After he punched me and I went home, we got together right here later that night to skip rocks. Even when we fought, neither of us ever stayed mad for very long. Anyway, he said to me that it'd be cool if I married you." Aiden's eyes cloud with unshed tears. "He told me I was already his brother, but that if we got married, it would make it official."

Even though I smile at his memory, tears fill my eyes. "He loved you. You were his brother in every way that mattered."

"The last time I saw him, he told me to get off my ass and go to you. He told me that, as my brother, he had the right to kick my ass for being stupid. Even when I didn't want to listen to him, he always swore we'd be right here someday. He always said that I'd officially be his brother someday."

"And I'm willing to bet he's toasting right now as he looks down on us."

"He's probably trying to figure out how to collect that fifty bucks I now owe him."

Laughter fills the night as Aiden and I hold each other, absorbed in the memories of Marcus and how we came to be in this moment. We went from best friends and young lovers to nothing at all but a memory. Then, tragedy struck. Losing Marcus was the hardest thing I've ever had to endure. But somehow, he managed to bring Aiden and me back together again.

And for that I will be forever indebted to my big, overprotective big brother.

A wise woman once said, sometimes love is right where you left it.

And, for me, my love is here. He's wrapped in my arms, showering me with eternal love.

He's the place I call home.

THE END

About the Author

Lacey Black is a Midwestern girl with a passion for reading, writing, and shopping. She carries her e-reader with her everywhere she goes so she never misses an opportunity to read a few pages. Always looking for a happily ever after, Lacey is passionate about contemporary romance novels and enjoys it further when you mix in a little suspense. She resides in a small town in Illinois with her husband, two children, and a chocolate lab. Lacey loves watching NASCAR races, shooting guns, and should only consume one mixed drink because she's a lightweight.

Email: laceyblackwrites@gmail.com
Facebook: https://www.facebook.com/authorlaceyblack
Twitter: https://twitter.com/AuthLaceyBlack
Blog: https://laceyblack.wordpress.com

Also by Lacey Black

Rivers Edge series
Trust Me, Rivers Edge book 1 (Maddox and Avery) – FREE at all retailers
~ *#1 Bestseller in Contemporary Romance & #3 in overall free e-books*
~ *#2 Bestseller in overall free e-books on another retailer*
Fight Me, Rivers Edge book 2 (Jake and Erin)
Expect Me, Rivers Edge book 3 (Travis and Josselyn)
Promise Me: A Novella, Rivers Edge book 3.5 (Jase and Holly)
Protect Me, Rivers Edge book 4 (Nate and Lia)
Boss Me, Rivers Edge book 5 (Will and Carmen)
Trust Us: A Rivers Edge Christmas Novella (Maddox and Avery)
~ *This novella was originally part of the Christmas Miracles Anthology*

Bound Together series
Submerged, Bound Together book 1 (Blake and Carly)
~ *An International Bestseller*
Profited, Bound Together book 2 (Reid and Dani)
~*A Bestseller, reaching Top 100 on 2 e-retailers*
Entwined, Bound Together book 3 (Luke and Sidney)

Lacey Black

Summer Sisters series
My Kinda Kisses, Summer Sisters book 1 (Jaime and Ryan)
	~*A Bestseller, reaching Top 100 on 2 e-retailers*
My Kinda Night, Summer Sisters book 2 (Payton and Dean)
My Kinda Song, Summer Sisters book 3 (Abby and Levi)

Standalone
Music Notes, a sexy contemporary romance standalone

*Coming Soon from Lacey Black
Book 4 in the Summer Sisters series, My Kinda Mess (Lexi and Linkin)

Made in the USA
Columbia, SC
23 December 2017